**KILLERS**

watched every move the Ranger ace made. Slade knew it. So he tensed to alertness as two shadowy figures approached in the poorly lit Juarez street.

They wore the hoods and flowing robes of brothers of the mission. But under the shorter robe of one Slade spotted—**a pair of rangeland riding boots!**

Slade's guns streaked from their holsters as the "brothers" whirled to face him. The quiet street exploded with gunfire. A slug ripped the crown of his hat. Then a stunning blow to his midriff sent him reeling—but both his guns pumped their lethal hail in the last seconds of a duel to the death!

BRADFORD SCOTT

KILLER'S DOOM

WILDSIDE PRESS

1 . . .

Ranger Walt Slade—whom the Mexican *peones* of the Rio Grande River villages named *El Halcón,* The Hawk —gazed at the words written on the scrap of paper Sheriff Arch Hart had drawn from his desk drawer. He read,

El *Halcón,* you will not catch Juan Covelo, but some day Juan Covelo will catch *you,* and then for you it will be *muy malo! muy malo!*

"The nerve of that sidewinder!" growled the sheriff. "Shovin' that thing under the office door sometime last night. Looks like he must have seen you riding in yesterday and stopping off here. Him or one of his hellions."

Slade studied the paper, turning it over and over in his slender, bronzed fingers.

"From the choice of words, the handwriting and the punctuation, I'd say Covelo is a man of some education," he commented.

"Uh-huh, mission taught, I expect," Hart agreed. "He's half white and half Yaqui Indian, or so I've heard."

"And apparently inherited all the vices and none of the virtues of both races," Slade observed.

"He sure did," replied Hart.

"Also has a flare for the bizarre and spectacular, which may prove his undoing," Slade said.

"Uh-huh, but don't underestimate him," warned the sheriff. "He means just what he says, and if he manages to drop a loop on you, it will be *muy malo* for you, very bad! Very bad! Remember what he did to Dick Combs when Dick tried to kill him and slipped up on the chore. Tied Dick up on top of a cliff where the vultures nest. Knife-slashed his face and left him. The vultures tackled Dick, like they will anything that's helpless and bleeding. Pecked out his eyes, tore open his throat and made a meal of him.

"And Wilbur Hayes, who had been sounding off against Covelo. I'll tell you what was left of Hayes when we found him. Covelo pegged him out over an ant hill, smeared him

5

with honey. Nothing much left but his skeleton when we found him, with the ants running in and out of his empty eye sockets. I heard Covelo sat and smoked cigarettes while the ants worked on Hayes. Oh, he's plumb sidewinder-poisonous. The only thing I ever heard of to touch him was the Karankawa Indians around Matagorda Bay. They were cannibals and usta boil folks alive. Said they tasted better with all the blood left in."

"Yes, the Kranks were somewhat salty," Slade conceded cheerfully. "But you'll have to admit that there was nothing personal in their method; it was based on what they held to be sound culinary procedure."

"You would have to make a joke about it!" snorted the sheriff. "But Juan Covelo ain't no joke, and don't you forget it."

"Sounds like a very interesting person," Slade replied. "And his streak of sadistic cruelty also may make him vulnerable. Well, we'll see," he added carelessly and began rolling a cigarette with the fingers of his left hand. Hart watched the operation and noted that not a crumb of tobacco was spilled.

"Sometimes think you haven't a nerve in your body," he complained. "'Here you're going up against the worst outlaw Texas has known since Veck Sosna, and you treat it as if it were a joke."

"Sosna finally got his comeuppance," Slade reminded him.

"Oh, sure you did for him, finally, but from the things you told me, it came darn near to going the other way a few times," the sheriff retorted.

"But it didn't," Slade returned blithely. "It's the cards you hold when all the chips are in that count; what went before were just trials of strength."

"I suppose so," Hart acceded wearily. "By the way, have you any notion he might know you are a Ranger?"

"I doubt it," Slade answered. "I think he figures you brought me in to run him down. Sheriffs have been known to hire professional gunslingers to do a chore for them, you know."

"Especially when they can't seem to do the chore themselves," admitted Hart. "That's why I wrote McNelty asking him to send you here. So you figure he thinks you're just *El Halcón,* 'the notorious outlaw too smart to get caught,' eh?"

That's about the size of it, in my opinion," Slade replied.

"*El Halcón,* 'the singingest man in the whole Southwest, with the fastest gunhand,' or so a lot of folks say about you."

"Both contentions open to debate," Slade observed smiling.

"I ain't so sure," grunted the sheriff. "Having heard you sing and having seen you in action, I'm inclined to go along with them. But did you ever think that the fastest gunhand part is a challenge to Covelo? He sets up to be no snide with an iron himself."

Slade smiled and did not otherwise comment.

"That blasted *El Halcón* foolishness is liable to get you into serious trouble sometime," the sheriff predicted morosely.

"Perhaps, but it also sometimes causes gentlemen like Juan Covelo to become careless, thinking that they have only one of their own brand to contend with," Slade pointed out. "Also, there is often loose talk in the presence of *El Halcón,* which would not be the case in the presence of a known Ranger."

This Sheriff Hart was forced to admit was so, although he shook his head pessimistically. As Captain Jim McNelty, the famous Commander of the Border Battalion of the Texas Rangers, often did after futilely reminding his lieutenant and ace-man of the risks involved.

"Can you give me a description of Covelo's personal appearance?" Slade asked.

The old sheriff shrugged his thin shoulders. " 'Pears nobody knows for sure just what he looks like," he replied. "Him and his hellions are always masked. I've got a half dozen different descriptions of the sidewinder from folks who thought they saw him and, the chances are, didn't. Seems he ain't very big, though just how big is hard to tell, for he always wears a long black hooded cloak or loose coat that mighty nigh covers him. I figure he's got a dark skin, seeing as he's half Yaqui."

Slade nodded agreement. "Yes, quite likely he has at least a swarthy complexion," he said. "That's generally the rule where there's an admixture of Yaqui blood, although of course not necessarily so. I've known Mexicans who had more than a dash who inherited the much fairer skin of their Spanish forbears. Know anything relative to his antecedents?"

"Not much," the sheriff admitted. "As I said, I understand he was mission taught. I heard his mother was a Yaqui princess, the daughter of a big chief, his father a sea captain."

"So Covelo is very likely not his real name," Slade interpolated.

"Chances are," the sheriff conceded. "When he robbed the bank at Orton—didn't kill anybody that time, because he didn't want to rouse up the town with a shooting, I reckon—one of the tellers was sure he had dark eyes. Oh, it was him, all right; he used his sorta trademark before he left—*Buenas noches Señor!*"

"Interesting in a way," Slade commented. "That was Joaquin Murrieta's closing salutation, which usually presaged the death of the person to whom it was addressed. Wonder how Covelo happened to hit onto it?" The sheriff raised his eyebrows.

"Murrieta?"

"Yes, the notorious California outlaw and killer; he was really bad."

"Figure he couldn't have been any worse than Covelo," Hart growled.

"Perhaps not," Slade admitted. "Just wait. Before long a yarn will be going the rounds that Covelo is Joaquin Murrieta back in business, even though he has been dead for years. I've known that sort of thing to happen a number of times with famous killers. And pretty soon folks begin to believe it and get scared accordingly."

"I'm about willing to believe anything," the sheriff declared gloomily.

"*Buenas noches, Señor,*" Slade repeated. " 'Goodnight, sir!' And it was generally 'goodnight' for the recipient of Murrieta's favor."

"And for Covelo's, too," said Hart.

Slade strolled to the window and gazed out at sun drenched Comanche Peak towering over El Paso, the city of the Pass to the North. Sheriff Hart gazed at him.

"What a fine looking feller," he murmured under his breath. "Never saw a finer."

Outlined in the golden glow, Slade did make a striking picture. Very tall, more than six feet, his wide shoulders and broad chest, slimming down to a lean, sinewy waist, were in keeping with his splendid height. His rather wide mouth, grin-quirked at the corners, relieved somewhat the tinge of fierceness evinced by the prominent hawk nose above and the powerful jaw and chin beneath. His pushed-back "J.B." revealed a wide forehead and thick, crisp hair so black a blue shadow seemed to lie upon it. The sternly handsome countenance was dominated by long, black-lashed eyes of very pale gray; cold, reckless eyes that nevertheless always seemed to have little devils of laughter lurking in their clear depths.

He wore the homely but efficient garb of the rangeland with the careless grace of a man who "becomes" his clothes, not them him, no matter what they are. The soft blue shirt, with vivid neckerchief looped at the throat, the well-worn "Levis" or bibless overalls and the scuffed half-boots of softly tanned leather were the customary habiliments of the cowhand.

Around his waist were double cartridge belts from the carefully worked and oiled cut-out holsters of which protruded the plain black butts of heavy guns; and from the butts of those big Colts his slender, powerful hands seemed never far away.

Turning from the window, Slade addressed the sheriff. "Any notion where Covelo might have his hang-out?"

The old peace officer shrugged again. "Some folks 'low it's south of the Rio Grande; I don't think so. Others say the Hueco Mountains over to the east of town, others the Malone Mountains down to the southwest. Just guess work. I've a prime notion that the devil spends quite a bit of his time here in El Paso."

"Quite likely," Slade agreed. "Here he could glean needed information he couldn't obtain elsewhere. But I'm of the opinion that he also has a secret hole-up where he can lie low for a spell when it is advisable to do so. For example, after such a foray as the bank robbery, he would hardly risk riding into town with his bunch. After a few days tucked away in security, they could drift in one or two at a time and attract no attention."

"Guess that's right," Hart admitted.

"Has he pulled anything lately?" Slade asked. The sheriff shook his head.

"Not for a couple of weeks, not since the bank job. Did pretty well there—close to thirty thousand dollars the hellion tied onto."

"Yes, a hefty haul, but if he has a pretty good sized bunch working with him, it won't last long. That sort lets money slip through their fingers mighty fast, and an outlaw leader must see to it that his followers are supplied with cash all the time if he hopes to keep his grip on them."

"Right again," said Hart. "He'll be on the move before long; you can bet your last peso on that. Oh, the devil! I'm hungry. Let's drop over to The Lookout on Kansas Street and tie onto a bite to eat."

"Suits me," Slade replied. They left the office and headed for the big combination saloon and restaurant.

Sheriff Hart's prediction was singularly accurate. Right then Juan Covelo was "on the move."

2 . . .

Old Tom Worthing, the driver of the Cornuda-El Paso stage, was rolling his clumsy vehicle through the hills. He had plenty on his hands keeping his four mettlesome horses from climbing the trees. With uncanny skill he swerved the cumbersome coach around hairpin turns, down steep sags, up winding slopes.

But just the same he had eyes for everything that went on around him. His gaze darted from the trail to the bristles of thicket, clumps of chimney rocks, huddles of boulders, and back again. Beside him sat an alert shotgun guard who also missed nothing. Another, equally watchful, sat in the boot behind. Neither Worthing nor the guards were taking any chances, for the stage packed a hefty passel of *dinero* in a strongbox inside the locked body of the coach. And it was known that Juan Covelo and his hellions had been operating in the section.

Not that Worthing was particularly worried. The guards were picked men, chosen for vigilance, cool-headedness and skill in gun handling. In addition to the double-barreled scatterguns loaded with buckshot across their laps, a rifle leaned against the knee of each, six-guns snuggled in their holsters. Worthing himself was heeled with a pair of Colts. Anybody making a try for the stage would be assured of a warm welcome.

Nevertheless, Worthing heaved a sigh of relief when the hills fell away on either side and the trail dipped to the level prairie where there was little cover, none at all close to the track. He relaxed on his seatbox. The guards relaxed a trifle also. The stage picked up speed on the level and surged forward with rumbling wheels, clicking hoofs and jingling harness. Nearly three hundred yards ahead was a clump of thicket, some distance from the trail, but otherwise the rangeland rolled free of vegetation other than the thickly grown carpet of grass.

Worthing glanced at the trail ahead and saw nothing to

disturb him. A keen observer like *El Halcón* might well have noted something that didn't look just right. Here and there little flecks of raw earth showed on the dusty gray surface.

But neither Worthing nor the guards possessed Walt Slade's marvelous eyesight or his meticulous observance and evaluation of all details no matter how small. The stage rolled on gaily, guards and driver chatting about the high old times they would have in El Paso that night. The stage rolled on, reached the stretch of peculiar looking trail.

Without preliminary warning there was a prodigious crackling and snapping. The two leaders plunged downward, screaming with fright. The wheelers catapulted over their scrambling forms in a wild tangle of hoofs, legs and broken harness. The front wheels of the coach surged down, the clumsy vehicle careened drunkenly. Guards and driver, with yells of alarm, clutched frantically at the iron railings as the coach lurched sideways, seemingly on the verge of overturning. Shotguns and rifles clattered to the floor boards. Everything was confusion and complete disarray.

From the thicket bulged a band of horsemen riding at top speed. As they neared the demoralized stage, guns blazed a deadly volley.

Riding somewhat in front was a man of medium height who looked taller because of a long black cloak that swathed his chest and shoulders and fell downward in graceful folds. Like his companions, he wore a black mask through holes in which his eyes gleamed darkly.

One of the guards, recovering from his moment of panic, stooped to retrieve his fallen shotgun. It was the last move he was to make on earth. His body lurched sideways, toppled over the railing and thudded into the hole in which the coach was mired. His companion, floundering on the tilted seat beside the driver, rose on his tiptoes and crashed forward onto the backs of the maddened horses that were trying desperately to climb out of the shallow excavation. Old Tom Worthing managed to get one of his six-guns from the holster, then he, too, fell soddenly to the dust of the trail, his face scarlet-visored by the blood that poured over it. Without sound or motion he lay, a grotesque huddle that seemed to say, "instant death!"

Up to the wrecked stage galloped the outlaws, eyes fixed on the motionless forms of guards and driver, guns ready for action. The cloaked leader swept the bodies with his gaze. "Dead!" was his verdict. "Get busy; I'll watch the trail."

A couple of shots and the door lock was smashed; the

door swung open. Working with speed and efficiency, the raiders hauled forth the strongbox. A couple more shots and its lock was broken. The contents were quickly removed, bills and coins, and stowed in saddle pouches. Then all mounted and raced away, heading west by south on the trail to El Paso.

As they rode off, the cloaked leader's voice sounded, clear and musical. Back to the scene of death drifted a mocking, *"Buenas noches, Señores!"*

As the band thundered away, old Tom Worthing's bloody head moved the merest trifle; his eyelids fluttered. A gleam showed between the lashes. Otherwise he lay without sign of life. Not until the outlaws were but bouncing blobs in the distance did he raise his bloodstained face from the dust. Groaning and gasping, he struggled to a sitting position and for several minutes sat with his head in his hands. Gradually his strength returned. He raised a trembling hand to the ragged gash across his left temple, explored it with a tentative fingertip, swore weakly at the sting.

"Skull ain't busted, anyhow," he muttered. "Just creased. Hit me one hell of a wallop, though. Take it easy, cayuses, I'll get you out of that mess in a minute; just let me rest a mite longer."

Finally he lurched to his feet, stood weaving for a moment, shaking his head and swearing. He tried a step or two, decided he still had enough left to make it. The splitting headache was abating, his vision clearing. He shook his head again, swore some more. For another moment he leaned against the body of the sagging coach. Then he fumbled a knife from his pocket and slashed at the tangled harness.

Once free, the horses, exhausted by their frantic struggles, scrambled weakly from the hole in the trail in which they had been trapped and stood blowing and snorting. Worthing had no trouble catching one and rigging a makeshift bridle. Then, after removing the others' bits, he forked the animal and, still muttering cuss words, headed it for El Paso. A single glance had convinced him there was nothing to be done for the two guards.

"Surround some grass, you jugheads," he called to the other horses. "Somebody will be along for you after a bit."

He still lurched a bit on the animal's back, but was in pretty good shape. He speeded up after a while and it did not take him long to cover the nearly ten miles to El Paso.

Slade and Hart had finished their meal and were enjoying a smoke over final cups of coffee when one of the sheriff's deputies rushed in breathing as if he had just done a fast mile. He spotted them and raced to the table, his eyes wild.

"What in blazes—" began Hart.

"Tom Worthing—the stage—he—he—he—" stuttered the deputy.

Sheriff Hart bellowed an oath. Slade spoke to the excited informant.

"Take it easy," he said. "Cool down and tell us what's the matter."

The quiet, musical voice and the force of the pale eyes fixed on his face calmed the deputy.

"Worthing shot, the guards killed, the stage robbed," he said. "Worthing figures Juan Covelo did it. He's over at the office."

"Tom badly hurt?" the sheriff asked anxiously.

"Not too bad, I guess," replied the deputy. "Head split open."

Slade was on his feet. "Let's go," he said. "You round up a doctor to look after Worthing," he told the deputy, who obeyed without question. Slade and the sheriff hurried to the office where they found Worthing sitting in a chair smoking his pipe and apparently little worse for his harrowing experience.

"Just a minute," Slade interrupted as he started to speak. "First I want to give your head a once-over."

With sensitive fingers, he explored the wound. "No fracture, I'd say," was his verdict. "I prefer not to express an opinion as to possible concussion; leave that for the doctor when he gets here. Now go ahead and tell us what happened."

The rugged old driver shot him a keen glance and then proceeded to unemotionally narrate his experience.

"Dug a hole in the trail, covered it with interlaced tree branches with dirt on top of the branches," he concluded. "We went into that hole hell-bent for election; darned near turned the stage over. Did just about turn us over. Before we could get untangled the devils were right on top of us. Poor Carter and Blake never had a chance. Reckon the hellions figured I was done for, too—I must have looked it."

Slade nodded but did not comment. "What makes you think it was Covelo and his bunch?" he asked.

"Well, the hellion who was giving the orders wore a long black cloak or something like it, like Covelo is said to wear, and when they rode off he hollered back, *'Buenas noches, Señores,'* " the driver replied.

"Oh, it was Covelo, all right," the sheriff interpolated.

"Possibly," Slade conceded. "Which way did they go?" he asked the driver.

"West on the El Paso trail," Worthing replied. "They kept to the trail till they were out of my sight. That might not have been too far, though; I wasn't seeing very good right then. Looked to me like they were headed for El Paso."

"Which was what they wanted it to look like, I'd say," Slade remarked.

"What do you mean?" asked the sheriff. "With them thinking everybody was done for."

Slade did not answer. Instead, he asked Worthing a question of his own that puzzled the sheriff.

"I suppose you were bleeding quite freely while you were lying on the ground?"

"Guess I was," Worthing admitted. "Blood kept running in my eyes. Why?"

"Dead men don't bleed," Slade answered dryly. "If it was Covelo and he's as smart as he is said to be, he would have very likely noticed that. In other words, he knew you were not dead but playing 'possum and rode west on the trail to throw off possible pursuit. After they were out of sight, they turned off somewhere, possibly backtracked east."

"By gosh, I bet you've hit it!" exclaimed the sheriff. "Would be just like the hellion. And I'd have fallen for it," he admitted. "I'd have been looking for the devils here in town or maybe over toward the Malones, or the Huecos."

"Exactly," Slade remarked. "Any notion how much of a haul they made?" he asked Worthing. The driver shook his head.

"All I know it was plenty," he replied. "Shipment to the bank here. Must have run into the thousands."

The doctor, a bearded old frontier practitioner, arrived at that moment. He shot Slade a quick glance and smiled slightly. Then he turned his attention to the injured driver for a quick examination as he dived into his bag for bandages and medicants.

"Nothing to it," he said. "I'll patch you up and then you can go and get drunk—will do you more good than anything else."

"That big feller said it didn't amount to much," remarked Worthing, gesturing to Slade.

"I've a notion he don't make many mistakes," said Doc McChesney, crinkling his eyes at Slade.

"You're darn right," seconded the sheriff.

Slade smiled and deftly changed the subject.

"Smart of the devils, waiting until you were out of the hills, onto the open range and feeling safe," he observed to the driver.

"Uh-huh, that's right," agreed Worthing, sucking hard on his pipe as Doc worked over him. "That belt of thicket, the only place they could hole up, was three hundred, maybe a mite more yards from the trail."

"Too great a distance to stage a successful corpse and cartridge session with a moving object," Slade commented. "Yes, your *amigo* Covelo, if it was him, is smart, all right. Just as smart, maybe more so than you made him out," he added to the sheriff, his eyes thoughtful, the concentration furrow deepening between his black brows, a sure sign that *El Halcón* was doing some hard thinking.

Sheriff Hart nodded and glanced out the window at the sun lying low in the western sky.

"Reckon we'd better mosey over there and collect the bodies before the coyotes tear 'em, and look after the stage horses. Guess we can make it by dark. No chance to track the hellions in the night, though."

Slade said nothing, but still looked thoughtful.

"Bob, go round up the boys, and four or five of the fellers who serve as specials," Hart told the deputy. "Better have a pretty good bunch along, just in case. Wouldn't you say so, Slade?"

"Yes, decidedly so," the Ranger answered, his eyes even more thoughtful. As they headed for their horses, he made a somewhat cryptic remark apropos of Juan Covelo.

"Yes, he's smart, perhaps even a bit smarter than he's given credit for being."

Sheriff Hart glanced at him inquiringly, but Slade did not elaborate at the moment.

"I'll never get over admirin' that critter; he's in a class by himself," the sheriff declared as Slade led Shadow, his splendid horse, from the stall. "Yes, in a class by himself."

Shadow was indeed worthy of admiration. Fully eighteen hands high, his lines bespoke great speed and equally great endurance. His glossy coat was midnight black, as was his glorious rippling name. His great liquid eyes were full of fire and intelligence. He whinneyed softly and rested his chin on Slade's shoulder.

"Anybody else try to touch him, without your permission, and he'd be short an arm," chuckled Hart. "Yep, in a class by himself."

"Old Shadow will do," Slade said as he deftly cinched the saddle into position and adjusted bit and bridle. "Well, the boys should be showing up by the time we reach the office; let's go."

The posse, eight strong, was awaiting them when they rode up to the office.

3 . . .

As the posse got under way, Slade said in low tones to the sheriff, "Drop behind."

Hart shot him a glance but did not argue. "What's on your mind?" he asked when the others were out of earshot.

"If I remember correctly," Slade replied, "about five miles from town the trail forks. A little used track on the left trends north by east, passing close to the Hueco tanks, where wind and rain erosion cut water holes in the soft granite. The Apaches holed up there and used it as a watering place. That trail turns south after a while and joins this trail again a couple of miles or so east of where the robbery occurred. Right?"

"Yes, that's right," agreed the sheriff. "I know that snake track well. Why?"

"When we reach the forks, we will take the trail to the north and follow it until it joins the El Paso," Slade said.

"But in the name of blazes, why?" demanded the bewildered peace officer.

"I'll tell you why," Slade answered. "As I said before, Juan Covelo may be just a mite smarter than even he is given credit for being. Evidently he knows *El Halcón*, and it is logical to believe that he knows how *El Halcón* thinks and works. I'm sure he'd figure that I'd guess his riding to the west toward El Paso was in the nature of a subterfuge, that I'd realize that he knew the driver wasn't dead and would relay the false information to me. He'd figure that I'd easily guess that he intended to circle back east toward the Hueco Mountains, presumably to take refuge in his hole-up there. Begin to get the notion?"

"No, blast it, I don't," retorted the sheriff. "We agreed that he'd circle back, but why should we go ambling off to the north and east? That I can't figure. If you're sure he headed east, why don't we head east?"

"Covelo circled back east all right," Slade said. "However, he didn't ride on to the Huecos, in my opinion. In-

17

cidentally, there will be a nearly full moon tonight, in a clear sky; excellent shooting light."

Sheriff Hart swore in exasperation. "Get to the nubbin' of the ear, won't you!" he growled. "What *is* on your mind?"

"If we rode up to the scene of the robbery, from the west, we'd all dismount and group around the bodies, wouldn't we?" Slade countered.

"The chances are we would," the sheriff admitted.

"And would be sitting ducks for rifle fire from the belt of thicket that Worthing, the driver, mentioned."

The sheriff sat bolt upright in his saddle. "You don't mean—"

"That's exactly what I mean," Slade interrupted. "I am of the opinion that Covelo surmised correctly just what my reaction to his westward ride away from the scene of the robbery meant. Correctly to an extent, but not quite far enough. I do not think that he suspects I guessed his real intention. In other words, I believe I'm a guess ahead of him, that he hasn't the least notion that I'm convinced that he and his bunch are holed up across from the El Paso trail in the edge of that broad and long belt of thicket. Holed up and waiting for us to come bulging along the trail in the bright moonlight. That's the premise on which I am banking. Instead of riding the El Paso trail, we will approach that belt of thicket from the north and east and, if we have good luck, perhaps turn the tables on *Señor* Covelo."

"By gosh!" exclaimed the sheriff. "I'm of the notion that you're right on all counts! The ornery sidewinder!"

"I could be wrong," Slade admitted, "But if I am we will have lost nothing—just been on a somewhat longer ride than we would have been otherwise."

"Uh-huh, and if you're right, which I believe you are, if we go skalleyhootin' over there like a bunch of loco mavericks, we may end up on a shorter ride but a helluva longer trip—the big jump! We'll do as you say."

"Okay," Slade nodded. "We'll move up and tell the boys; you do the talking."

Sheriff Hart did so, without preamble. "When we come to the fork, we turn north," he said.

The men stared at him in astonishment; some voiced a protest. Sheriff Hart quickly stemmed the outburst.

"Slade says to do it that way, and that's the way we're going to do it," the sheriff declared conclusively.

The posse regarded Slade's tall form, and his eyes, and gave way without further argument.

When they reached the fork, Slade called a halt. In a few terse sentences he explained his plan. The men stared at him; some whistled under their breath.

"Blazes!" exclaimed one. "Feller, I believe you're right, and if it wasn't for you, us loco jugheads would have bulged right over there and got blowed from under our hats."

"Perhaps," Slade agreed. "Anyhow, we're not taking the chance. Let's go!"

They turned left and rode at a fast pace. The moon had risen and was flooding the rangeland with silvery light. Thickets and clumps of brush stood forth in bold relief, their shadows as solid as the growth itself. Slade estimated the distance and after some time had passed, he again called a halt.

"A little less than a mile ahead this track joins the El Paso trail again," he said. "Right, Sheriff?"

"That's right," replied Hart.

"So here we turn back west by south," Slade said. "Something over a mile should bring us opposite that belt of thicket where the hellions holed up to wait for the stage. We'll ease south to the thicket. Then I'll try and figure what's what."

Turning their horses, they rode on and before long the keen eyes of *El Halcón* sighted the shadowy loom a half mile or so distant that he knew was the thicket. Once more he called a halt and sat studying the ominous belt of growth.

"They're there," he announced.

"How the devil do you know?" demanded Hart. "I sure can't see anything."

"I can't see anything, either, but I can hear," Slade answered, still gazing toward the thicket.

"What?"

"The coyotes," Slade explained. "Everywhere to the east, the north, the west they are yipping, baying at the moon. But from that thicket, where one would expect them to be prowling the edges of the growth, there comes no sound of barking. Which means that there's something in there the little wolves are afraid of; and it's logical to believe that the something has two legs, not four."

"Darned if you ain't right again," growled Hart. "You're the limit! Now what?"

"Now," Slade said, "we'll walk our horses to this edge of the thicket, hoping the canny devil hasn't posted a watchman on this side of the belt. In which case we'll very likely get a hot reception."

The posse swore, individually and collectively, and stiffened in the saddles.

"I don't think you need to get overly jumpy," Slade added, with a chuckle. "I'm pretty sure there will be nobody on this side of the thicket; if they are in there, I'd say they'll all be concentrating on the trail and would hardly pay any attention to the prairie over here. At least that's the logical deduction as I see it. Walk your horses, and keep your bit irons quiet. I believe the stage driver said the robbery occurred opposite just about the middle of the thicket. So we'll veer just a little to the west and hit the center of it. Let's go."

It was nerve-wracking work, moving slowly across the open prairie in the still, white flood of the moonlight. The deputies were plain scared, and even *El Halcón* was not as comfortable as he might have been; Covelo had proven himself a shrewd reasoner. Maybe he had guessed a little farther ahead than he, Slade, anticipated; maybe he had made the last guess. Well, they'd find out shortly.

On and on, slowly, silently. The distance seemed interminable, the belt of thicket no closer. To Slade's vivid imagination it seemed to be walking away from them. But the more than six hundred yards of distance shrank to four, to three, to one. Now they were in perfect shooting position for anybody holed up in the brush. Slade realized he was holding his breath. He exhaled angrily. Fifty yards more to go; looked like his was the last guess, after all. But with his companions he breathed a sigh of relief when they drew rein at the edge of the growth. Slade motioned the others to dismount and gather around him.

"We'll have to leave the horses here," he whispered. "I hope they don't go singing any songs and will stand."

"They'll stand," breathed the sheriff. "They're well-trained critters, and they'll be quiet."

"Okay," Slade returned. "We're going through that brush to the other side, in single file, each man with his hand on the shoulder of the man in front. I'll lead, Hart next to me. When I want you to fan out on either side, ready for business, I'll reach back and touch Hart. He'll touch the man behind him and so on down the line. If we can execute the maneuver without making a racket, we should be all set with the advantage of surprise on our side. I'm pretty sure it'll come to a shooting, so make every shot count. Everything understood? Let's go."

They eased into the growth. Slade took each forward

step with cat-like feet, making sure there was no dry branch to tread on, no stone to kick, no unexpected depression. Behind him the line of deputies moved with the greatest caution. They were men used to such a terrain and made no mistakes.

Gradually Slade became conscious of a sound, a murmuring that grew to a mutter, which he quickly identified as the voices of men talking among themselves. To his sensitive nostrils drifted the tang of cigarette smoke. The devils were there, all right, and being able to see for a great distance along the trail, they did not need to be cautious. He ground his teeth together in hot anger. The murderous snakes deserved no mercy. But he was a law enforcement officer and a Texas Ranger and must give them a chance to surrender.

A score more of slow, cautious steps; the growth was thinning. Another moment and he saw the outlaws, thirteen of them, grouped together just beyond the last fringe of brush, smoking and chatting, clearly outlined in the moonlight. He halted, reached back and touched Sheriff Hart. There followed the faintest rustling as the deputies fanned out. Everything was going like clockwork.

And then it happened! One of the slowly moving deputies stepped in to a leaf-filled marmot hole. He made a frantic grab at an overhead branch to save himself from falling. The branch was dry and rotten and broke with a crack like a pistol shot in the great silence. The deputy crashed into a clump of brush. He was carrying a cocked gun in his hand and managed to let that go off with a thunderclap boom.

The outlaws, volleying exclamations, whirled about and went for their guns.

"Let them have it!" Slade roared, and shot with both hands. The brush jumped and quivered to a veritable burst of tremendous sound. Yells of pain, curses, shouts, the bellowing of the guns rose to the shuddering stars. Three of the owlhoots went down at the first volley. Slade heard a yelp on one side of him, a gulping grunt on the other and knew that some of his companions had caught it. He continued to fire as fast as he could pull the trigger at the ducking, dodging, weaving shapes outlined in the moonlight. Two more men fell, and still another. The remainder dashed madly down the line of growth, shooting as they ran. Slade leaped from cover, caught sight of a cloaked figure leading the rout. His gun jutted forward.

But at that instant a slug grazed his temple and hurled

him sideways with the shock. Bells clanged in his ears, lights blazed before his eyes. His vision cleared almost instantly, but by the time he recovered, the cloaked figure he reasoned was Juan Covelo was nowhere in sight. He bounded forward and heard a prodigious crashing in the brush. The outlaws had reached their horses and were fleeing through the growth where the posse could not line sights with them. Another moment and they flashed into view more than a hundred yards to the east.

Slade emptied his guns after them, saw a man lurch wildly but keep his seat. The deputies and the sheriff were blazing away at the racing owlhoots, but with no success.

"To the horses!" Slade shouted and tore through the growth, heedless of thorns and trailing branches. But when he reached the far edge, he halted with a disgusted oath and began replacing the spent shells in his guns with fresh cartridges.

4 . . .

Shadow was right where Slade had left him, but the other horses, frightened by the uproar, had scattered over the prairie and stood several hundred yards away, blowing and snorting. Before they could be rounded up, the outlaws would have such a start as to make pursuit futile. On Shadow he might possibly overtake them, but odds of six or seven to one were a bit lopsided even for *El Halcón*.

The deputies came straggling from the brush, one limping badly, another cherishing a bullet-slashed arm.

"Just nicks," Sheriff Hart said cheerfully. "The hellions couldn't see us holed up in the brush and just cut loose at random, as it was. But it gives me the shakes to think of what would have happened if we'd come bouncing along that open trail in the moonlight. You sure saved our bacon."

Slade's first thought was for the wounded. A quick examination revealed that their hurts, while painful, were not serious. He went to work on the injured with medicants from his saddle pouches. Soon the wounds were smeared with antiseptic salve and were padded and bandaged, the bleeding retarded.

"That should hold you till Doc McChesney can look you over," he told them.

"Reckon no sawbones could do a better chore than you have," declared one of the injured, puffing hard on a cigarette. "Don't happen to be one, do you?" Slade smiled and shook his head.

Meanwhile the others had retrieved the horses and were grouped about, smoking and talking.

"Suppose we go see what we bagged," suggested the sheriff. "We got some of the devils, all right."

Leading the horses, they wormed their way through the growth to the scene of the fight. Six bodies were scattered over the ground.

"Not bad, not bad at all," chuckled Hart as the carcasses were turned over on their backs for examination. A heap of dry branches was kindled to aid the moonlight and the posse gathered around.

"Strip off those black rags and let's see what they look like," suggested the sheriff.

The masks were removed to disclose hard-bitten countenances with nothing particularly outstanding about them so far as Slade could see. The deputies peered close.

"Say!" exclaimed one, "I've seen this little scrawny hellion, in town. I remember him from the birthmark on his cheek that looks like somebody had walloped him good. Sure, I've seen him, hanging around the saloons down by the river."

Another deputy uttered an exclamation. "And I've seen this big one," he declared. "Down around the river, too. Looks like those rum holes are a sorta hangout for the bunch."

"Could be," Slade agreed.

"Yes, we didn't do bad," repeated the sheriff as he began turning out the dead men's pockets to reveal odds and ends of little interest and quite a bit of money, which he confiscated. "Not bad at all—six of the devils. I believe you said you counted thirteen, didn't you, Walt? Nearly half. Just half, without including the he-wolf, Covelo."

"Yes, without counting Covelo," Slade commented. "I notice none of these is wearing a black cloak. Covelo got away, which means we still have trouble on our hands." He fingered one of the masks.

"By the way, does Covelo usually kill everybody when he makes a raid?" he asked of Hart, who shook his head.

"Nope, usually somebody doesn't catch it, at least not more than an air hole in his hide," he replied.

"And from those that escaped death, you always got the same description of the bunch, eh? All masked, with one, presumably Covelo, wearing a long black cloak."

"Guess that's right," Hart admitted.

"Which means you get no real description that is worth anything," Slade commented. "I've a notion Covelo purposely allows one to escape, if possible. To escape and bring in that description, which is all you ever have to go on, which means nothing at all. The black masks and the black cloak are indelibly stamped on folks' minds, which is just what Covelo wants to happen. Oh, he's shrewd, all right. And I think he considers still another angle."

"What's that?"

"A long black cloak and black masks are fast becoming symbols of terror in the section," Slade explained. "Which is going to result in another unpleasant development which Covelo counts on. Very soon, I fear, you are going to have a plenitude of black cloaks and black masks. Every stray owl-hoot with a few brush poppers at his back is going to imitate Covelo. It always happens that way. Which won't make running down the real Covelo any easier."

The sheriff swore wearily and 'lowed it was very likely so.

From down the line of growth sounded a plaintive whinny.

"Hello!" Slade exclaimed. "Looks like these hellions' horses were left behind."

"Go see," said the sheriff to a deputy who hurried along the edge of the thicket, listening and peering.

"Here they are," he called a moment later. "Hitched to branches just inside the brush. What shall I do with them?"

"Bring them here," the sheriff called back. "Go help him, a couple of you fellers."

When the horses, good looking animals, were brought into the circle of firelight, Slade studied the brands and shook his head.

"I don't recognize any of them," he announced. "Rigged burns, I'd say, that won't be found in any authentic brand book; an old owlhoot trick. Well, we can use the critters to pack the bodies back to town. Guess we might as well be moving; I for one am hungry."

There was general agreement as to that and the deputies began hoisting the bodies onto the horses and roping them in place. Slade meanwhile was examining the contents of the saddle pouches. From one he drew forth packets of bills of large denomination and rolls of gold coins.

"Look," he called to Hart. "We did even better than we figured; we've also recovered part, at least, of the robbery money. Examine those other pouches."

Two of the pouches revealed more money, a lot of it. The sheriff chortled with delight.

"I've a notion Covelo is fit to be tied about now," he said. "Looks like he lost a good part of the loot. Yep, we did all right. And I want all you fellers to understand," he added, "that the credit goes to Slade."

"Who also saved our worthless hides for us," one of the deputies remarked. A point nobody argued.

The stage horses were easily located, grazing not far from the wrecked vehicle. Onto them were loaded the bodies of the murdered guards.

The cavalcade got under way. Two of the deputies, bringing up the rear, conversed.

"Just who the devil is that big feller, Slade?" one, a comparative newcomer to the section, asked.

"Don't you know?" replied his companion. "That's *El Halcón.*"

"*El Halcón?*"

"Uh-huh, that's what the Mexican *peones* named him. *El Halcón*, The Hawk. Name sorta fits, don't it? He sorta reminds you of one of those big gray mountain hawks that'll give an eagle his comeuppance. Lots of folks will tell you he's an outlaw himself, too smart to get caught, and sorta on the prod against other owlhoots. I ain't sayin' anything as to that."

The other whistled under his breath. "Sheriff Hart sure caters to him," he remarked. "Does just what he says to do and don't arg'fy."

"The same went for Sheriff Serby, who retired last year," said the other deputy. "Him and Slade were mighty friendly. And Hart's brother, who's sheriff of Hudspeth County, swears by him, too. 'The singingest man in the whole Southwest, with the fastest gunhand,' they say of him."

"Don't know about the singing part, not having heard him warble, but I sure won't arg'fy the gun angle," said the first speaker. "I was standing beside him there in the brush when he pulled his irons. Never saw anything like it. Wouldn't have thought such speed was possible. One second his hands were empty, the next they were filled with death and destruction. And I figure he downed at least three of the six we did for. And when the rest of the bunch were two hundred yards away and skalleyhootin' like scared coyotes, he winged one and nigh knocked him outa the hull. With a six-gun in the moonlight, that's some shooting!

"Somehow, I don't go for the owlhoot angle," the newcomer concluded, "but whether he is or whether he ain't, for my money he's a man to ride the river with."

The other nodded sober agreement. "And," he said, "he's the first jigger to make any headway against Juan Covelo."

The newcomer spat pensively at a lizard "mooning" itself on a rock and drowned old scaly-toes in a flood of amber tobacco juice.

"I think," he said as the disgusted lizard swam out and went away from there, "that Juan Covelo is mighty nigh to the end of his twine."

As he rode, Slade turned in the saddle to gaze back at the dark loom of the Hueco Mountains, their towering crests glittering where the moonlight was reflected from the naked rock. He wondered if Juan Covelo really had a hidden hole-up in their rugged fastnesses.

It seemed fairly logical, though of course not certain. The Huecos were but little more than twenty miles from El Paso, easy riding distance. The mountains were readily accessible by way of the trail that ran through Hueco Pass to cross the weird and desolate area called the Salt Flats and on through Guadalupe Pass, Guadalupe Canyon and on to the New Mexico Line. A little travelled trail, almost never used during the hours of darkness.

Sheriff Hart had mentioned the Malone Mountains as a possible location, but Slade thought otherwise. The Malones were more than fifty miles south by east from El Paso and could be reached only by way of a much more travelled trail. Yes, the Huecos were the logical terrain. That is unless Covelo's real hole-up was south of the Rio Grande, in Mexico.

Be that as it may, he was convinced that the wily outlaw's real base of operations was El Paso itself. Well, it was up to him to find out. He turned his face west and rode on in a cheerful frame of mind for he felt that already he had accomplished something. He had outguessed Covelo and, as the saying goes, had stolen a march on the miscreant. With the loss of six of his followers and quite likely what was a good portion of the stage robbery proceeds, Covelo must have suffered a considerable jolt. Perhaps as was the beginning, so would be the end.

It was late when they reached El Paso, for progress with the burdened led horses was slow, but there were plenty of people still on the streets. And very quickly there was plenty of excitement. A crowd gathered and followed the grim cavalcade to the courthouse, asking questions that nobody had time to answer.

"You fellers stay outside," the sheriff ordered. "We'll talk to you later."

The bodies were unroped and packed into the office, where they were laid out on the floor.

"Can't move for carcasses," grumbled the sheriff. "Guess it could be worse, though; we might have had to lay out ourselves."

"That would have been something of a chore, but I get what you mean," Slade commented.

"Now what?" Hart asked.

Slade motioned the wounded men to chairs. "Now send somebody to fetch Doc McChesney, and somebody else to round up the bank cashier and bring him here," he directed.

Sheriff Hart at once dispatched deputies to attend to the chores.

"The rest of you fellows can go out and tell the crowd what happened, before they topple over from curiosity," Slade told the remaining deputies. He sat down and rolled a cigarette. Sheriff Hart filled his pipe.

White-bearded old Doc McChesney had anticipated the call and strolled in a moment later.

"Figured I'd be needed when you hellions rode out of town," he said, with a meaningful glance at Slade. "You say you patched 'em up? Okay, I'll look 'em over, but it'll just be a waste of time."

He proceeded to do so, putting on fresh pads and bandages, which he replaced exactly as he found the ones Slade had applied.

"That'll hold you," he said, straightening his back. "Go get drunk." He turned to Hart. "Now suppose you tell me just what happened, Arch."

Sheriff Hart did so, and the story lost nothing in the telling, especially the part Slade played. Old Doc did not look in the least surprised, and repeated the comment of the newcomer deputy who drowned the lizard, not exactly word for word but identical in sentiment. "I've a notion that very shortly Juan Covelo is due to be a gone goslin'." The sheriff and the deputies nodded emphatic agreement.

However, Slade was not so optimistic. Covelo had lost a skirmish, that was all. Very likely right now the resourceful devil was planning to even the score, and *El Halcón* felt that unless he himself stepped lively Covelo might well do it.

"Inquest at two o'clock," said Doc, who was the coroner. He snapped his bag shut and departed. The two bandaged deputies shuffled after him, doubtless bent on following his advice, and headed for the nearest saloon—doctor's orders!

A few minutes later, John Knolles, the bank cashier, arrived. He checked over the money retrieved from the dead outlaws' saddle pouches and nodded approval.

"Near as I can figure, you recovered something better than half the shipment," he announced. "Which was a devil of a lot more than we expected to see. Congratulations! And I expect the insurance company will have a little present for you fellows. Thank you, Mr. Slade, very much. I gathered from the deputy that you were the chief moving force in the venture."

"He was all of that, whatever the devil you're talking about," said the sheriff. The cashier chuckled and took his leave with the money, the deputy accompanying him, just in case.

"And now what?" asked Hart.

"Now," replied Slade, "suppose we go and tie onto something to eat, and then bed."

"I'm in favor of it," agreed the sheriff. "Beginning to feel a mite tuckered; it's been a hard day. But a sorta good one, thanks to you," he added as he locked the office door.

5 . . .

In his comfortable hotel room, Slade slept soundly until nearly noon. He bathed and shaved and enjoyed a leisurely breakfast. After which he repaired to the sheriff's office to kill time until the inquest was held.

The inquest was short, the jury's verdict terse and to the point. The two guards met their death at the hands of persons unknown, six of whom, it appeared, had been properly taken care of. The sheriff was urged to run down the rest of the devils without delay. The six outlaws got just what was coming to them.

"Now what do you figure to do?" Hart asked as he and Slade left the coroner's office together.

"I think I'll prowl around town for a while, especially down by the river, where one is most likely to hear something of interest."

"Guess that's right," conceded Hart. "Some new places down there since you were here last. Feller named Gus Hansen opened up one about six months back, on South Santa Fe Street. Gave it a sort of loco name—Lemming Inn."

Slade chuckled. "I would say that Mr. Hansen, who is doubtless of Norse descent, has a somewhat bizarre sense of humor," he commented. "The lemmings are little rodents that inhabit the Arctic regions of both hemispheres and Norway. The Norweigian lemming is famous for its migrations. At intervals vast swarms leave their homes in the central mountains of Scandinavia. Millions of them travel west; nothing can stop them. They continue straight to the sea, into which they plunge and are drowned. A striking example of mass suicide, as it were. I don't know whether Mr. Hansen chose the name as a gentle hint to his patrons to behave, or because of his place's proximity to the river."

"Still sounds loco to me," grunted the sheriff. "But Hansen does run an orderly place and everything is on the up-and-up, so far as I have been able to ascertain. Town Marshal thinks so, too. Four or five doors from Hansen's place is another new rum hole I ain't so sure of. Feller who calls himself Joe Brian, though he looks more Mexican to me than Irish, opened that one about a month or so after Hansen set up in business. He's a hard looking customer and a sorta rough crowd goes there. I've been keeping an eye on that joint, but so far I haven't noticed anything really off-color."

"Both sound interesting," Slade said. "I think I'll give them a whirl. What's the name of Brian's place?"

"The Tank," answered Hart. "Sorta fits."

Slade chuckled again and left the office.

Slade liked El Paso and he wandered about the town quite a bit before turning his steps toward the river. The afternoon was well along when he located The Tank and sauntered in to occupy a table from which he had a clear view of the swinging doors and could study the room as reflected in the mirror behind the bar.

The place didn't look bad, he thought. The furnishings were not expensive, but everything was clean and well cared for, the long bar, the lunch counter, the two roulette wheels, a faro bank, tables for gaming, the dance-floor, now unoccupied, that was neither small nor large. There were quite a few patrons at the bar and scattered about at the tables. Some salty looking specimens among them, he decided, but not outstandingly so.

At the far end of the bar, close to the till, was an individual he rightly judged to be Joe Brian, the owner.

Brian was a man of medium height and slender build, but wiry looking and well set up. Slade readily saw why Sheriff Hart maintained that Brian looked more Mexican than Irish. His complexion was quite dark, his eyes black and snapping, his hair as black as Slade's own, his teeth as white as Slade's but somewhat crooked instead of being straight and even.

Studying his features, Slade formed his own opinion as to Brian's ancestry.

A waiter with a pleasant smile served the Ranger, who sat sipping his drink and surveying the room and its occupants.

A rough looking character shuffled down the bar to where Joe Brian stood and said a few words to the owner, who immediately turned and glanced in Slade's direction. A moment later he approached the table.

"Mr. Walt Slade, is it not?" he asked in a deep but not unpleasant voice. Slade intimated that he was right.

"The boys have been talking about you, and one of them

just pointed you out to me," said Brian. "Mind if I join you for a moment?"

"Certainly not," Slade replied. "Take a load off your feet and be comfortable."

"Thank you," Brian acknowledged and drew up a chair. He motioned the waiter to bring drinks.

"Yes, we've been hearing quite a bit about you today, and all to the good," he resumed. "You are to be congratulated, Mr. Slade. Sheriff Hart needs a deputy like you."

"I've a notion he has been doing very well," Slade observed.

"Against the average brand of lawbreakers, but that pest Covelo is something quite different from the average."

"Presumably."

Brian's eyes narrowed the merest trifle. "You knew Sheriff Hart before?" he asked.

"Yes."

"Worked with him before?"

"No."

Brian looked baffled. He was learning what others had learned before him. That Walt Slade would talk, freely and pleasantly, but he wouldn't tell you anything. After a few random remarks he rose to his feet and motioned the waiter to refill Slade's glass.

"Hope you'll see fit to visit us often, Mr. Slade," he said. "Sort of boisterous here now and then, but the boys don't mean any harm and usually everybody has a good time."

"Thank you," Slade said smilingly. Brian nodded and strode back to the end of the bar. His head bartender eyed him expectantly.

"Well, did you learn anything?" he asked.

"Nothing," Brian returned shortly. "He's *El Halcón,* all right, no doubt as to that. He tallies perfectly with Blount's description of *El Halcón,* but that's as far as I could get. He answers questions in a manner that leaves you right up in the air. I can usually draw a man out with indirect questions, but not him. When I left off it was right where I began. I wonder just what is his real reason for coiling his twine here?"

The bartender shrugged. "Well, you've heard of *El Halcón*'s reputation for horning in on good things other folks have started, and ending up skimming off the cream or something very like that. Could be here."

"Sheriff Hart 'pears to think well of him," Brian remarked musingly. The barkeep shrugged again.

"Hart's grabbing at anything that may 'pear to improve

conditions here and get him off a hot spot with election coming up soon," he observed sententiously.

"Well, anyhow, he'll sure bear watching," Brian said.

"You're darn right," agreed the drink juggler.

Slade could not hear the conversation, but he had a very good notion as to just what was the subject. There was an amused gleam in his cold eyes. Mr. Brian, of course, had been indulging in a little genteel probing, and had gotten exactly nowhere. No doubt but that he was quite interested in *El Halcón* and would very much like the answers to certain questions relative to that enigmatic individual. Which answers he hadn't gotten so far.

Meanwhile, Slade had been studying Brian. An able man of above average intelligence and with some education, was his conclusion. Somewhat different from the usual riverfront saloonkeeper. Which was something to keep in mind. Sheriff Hart had expressed himself somewhat dubious relative to Brian and the old peace officer was shrewd and usually a pretty good judge of men.

However, Slade was seldom swayed by the expressed opinions of others; he preferred to draw his own conclusions. He beckoned the waiter and ordered sandwiches and coffee.

The sun had set, the dusk was falling, and The Tank was filling up. Dawdling over his sandwiches and coffee, Slade studied the crowd. More rather rough looking customers were dropping in. Nothing out of the ordinary for a riverfront saloon, however, so far as he could ascertain. There were quite a few cowhands, others who were undoubtedly rivermen, some Mexican *vaqueros*.

Some of the gentlemen in rangeland garb Slade shrewdly suspected would quite likely not be able to show recent marks of rope or branding iron on their hands. Nothing unusual about that, however. El Paso was a crossroads and entertained all sorts.

He also suspected that there was plenty of potential dynamite present although at the moment the atmosphere was peaceful and everybody seemed to be having a good time. He also had a notion that Joe Brian and his floor men were well able to handle any trouble that might develop.

After a while, Slade beckoned the waiter, settled his score and strolled out. Slanting a glance at the bar mirror, he saw Brian and the bartender, their heads together, following his progress with their eyes. He smiled thinly and walked on until he reached the Lemming Inn, nearer the bridge, favorably mentioned by Sheriff Hart.

The Lemming Inn was more pretentious than The Tank, the furnishing in better taste, the lighting adequate, and it was quieter. It gave an impression of solidity and permanence, as it it were here to stay. Slade thought that very likely the case, the location being good and El Paso a growing town.

The patrons, so far as he could see, differed little from those of The Tank, with the exception of some well-dressed and prosperous looking individuals Slade surmised were ranch owners or local shopkeepers. He located a table and ordered a drink.

Here the dance-floor was already occupied and the girls, Slade thought, were not at all bad. And the Mexican orchestra was really good.

He noted, incidentally, there were more Mexicans here than at The Tank, the majority of them well-dressed and prosperous looking. Evidently the Lemming Inn got the upper crust of the owners and employees along the river streets.

As Slade sipped his drink, a man entered, cast a swift glance around the room and walked lithely to the far end of the bar next to a closed door that doubtless led to a back room. A bartender hurried to greet him. Slade wondered who the man was. He was enlightened a moment later.

"That's the boss who just came in, Mr. Hansen," said the waiter at his elbow, a cheerful and loquacious individual. "He owns the diggin's. Been away for a coupla days."

Slade nodded and surveyed Hansen with interest. He was a well set up man, rather slender but with wide shoulders and a broad chest. His complexion was the clear bronze attained by blonde coloring exposed to wind and weather. His eyes were dark blue, his hair yellow, with the lamp light reflecting gleams of gold. A fine looking man, Slade thought, with his straight and comely features and his square chin.

All in all, he reminded the Ranger of pictures of the Vikings he had seen, except for the lack of the fierce and drooping mustaches which were usually a part of the personal adornment of those gentry. Give him chain mail and a big battle-ax and he would be perfect! Slade chuckled at the thought; such accouterments would hardly be fitting for a riverfront saloonkeeper who quite probably had never heard of a Viking, although his name hinted at Norse forbears.

For a while Hansen conferred with his head bartender, glancing at papers the other passed him. Finally, with a wave of his hand he dismissed the drink juggler and began moving about the room, pausing for a word with groups or individuals. He had a smile for the dance-floor girls, a nod for the orchestra. Ultimately he worked around to Slade's table, paused and said with a pleasant smile, "Good evening, sir, first time here?"

"That's right," Slade replied.

"Glad to have you," Hansen said. "Always welcome strangers, hoping they won't stay strangers but will come back. That's what this business depends on, folks that come back."

"Seems to be doing pretty well," Slade commented, glancing about the busy room.

"Yes, not bad," Hansen conceded. "I hope to do better as time goes on."

"Logical to think that you will," Slade answered.

"I hope so," Hansen said. "Took me quite a while to save up enough to get into business for myself. But I really believe I'll make a go at it. Make yourself at home, now. I'll send over a drink."

"I'll settle for a cup of coffee, if you don't mind," Slade differed.

"Certainly," Hansen replied, beckoning the waiter. "Anything you wish." With a smile and a nod he sauntered back to the end of the bar. A moment later, a sheaf of papers in his hand, he opened the door Slade had noticed and passed through it, closing it behind him. Very likely going to settle down to a session of checking stock.

"He's all right," said the waiter, when he brought the coffee. "Nice to everybody, good to the help. But he won't stand for any foolishness. Says he aims to run a square and orderly place that'll attract the right sort of people, or know the reason why. Reckon he means it."

Slade was inclined to think the waiter had the right of it. He was of the opinion that Gus Hansen could be plenty salty if necessary.

Hansen was impeccably garbed, his ruffled shirt front snow against his black coat. Neither gun nor cartridge belt was in evidence, but the keen eyes of *El Halcón* had noted a slight bulge beneath his left armpit; the Lemming Inn proprietor was a shoulder holster man.

After lingering a bit longer over his coffee and a cigarette, Slade said goodnight to the friendly waiter and left the Lemming Inn. He chuckled as his eyes rested on the lettering across the wide window, done in pale green, the color of a shallow sea under the sun. Symbolical, perhaps. Gus Hansen undoubtedly had a sense of humor and quite likely enjoyed his little joke.

Outside, Slade paused, uncertain which way to turn. Overhead, nearby, the bridge loomed against the stars, a tracery of shadows etched in silver. He decided to cross the river to El Paso's sister city, Juarez, to the south in Mexico.

6 . . .

Slade liked Juarez. Here the gaiety was just as effervescent but held a softer, mellower note. Juarez always seemed to exude an effluvium of age and the placidity of age; an old *hombre* drowsing in the sun.

Not that it couldn't be lively at times; it had known stirring days and its streets had echoed to the rattle of gunfire, in war or otherwise, and would again. Also, it was frequented by gentlemen of easy morals who had found it expeditious to leave Texas and other points north for a while. These tried their best to keep things from growing dull, and succeeded. Young and exuberant *vaqueros* from the great ranches to the south and young and equally exuberant cowhands from north of the Rio Grande also did their best. Juarez absorbed them all, and asked for more.

Slade was not altogether pleasure bound in his decision to visit Juarez. The Mexican town was in the nature of a clearinghouse for news of what went on along the border. There was a chance, he felt, that he might learn something relative to the activities of Juan Covelo. Little doubt but that the bandit leader visited Juarez at times, and Slade had not dismissed the possibility that he might have a hang-out south of the Rio Grande. He didn't really think so, but it was best not to pass up any bets. Covelo was an unpredictable hellion and could reasonably be counted on to do the unexpected.

In the middle of the span he paused a moment to gaze back at El Paso, a necklace of light-diamonds clasping the throat of night, with the black and rugged bulk of Comanche Peak glowering down at the City of the Pass. To the south the lights were also bright, but more scattered. He continued on his way.

Always the first sound that greeted one's ears upon leaving the south approach of the bridge was the sound of music. It drifted through the doors and open windows of the *cantinas*, from the thatched and flat-roofed houses of the poorer residents, and mingled with subdued laughter and languid mur-murings, from patches of shadow beneath the trees. Wandering troubadours gathered at street corners, strumming their guitars and singing the folk songs of *Mejico*. Dressed in *charro* costumes, including gay *sombreros*, embroidered *serapes* and velvet pantaloons, the serenaders were always the center of a throng that lustily carroled the choruses. Juarez was a kaleidescopic melody rising to the blossoming stars.

Slade walked warily as he strolled about the town, for he believed that his every movement was very likely watched by killers who just awaited opportunity. He rather hoped it was the case, and that he might be able to provide "oppor-tunity" that could possibly provide *him* with some informa-tion relative to Juan Covelo, or even contact with that slippery individual.

Finally he found himself traversing a poorly lighted and practically deserted side street away from the business sec-tion. He tensed to alertness as he spotted two figures coming toward him, then relaxed. The two men wore the hoods and the flowing robes of brothers of the mission which had its headquarters in the town. Their eyes glinted sideways toward him but they swept past without speaking. Perhaps they were under a vow of silence. He half turned, his glance following their progress. He was about to turn back when his keen eyes noticed something that didn't look just right. His guns were streaking from the holsters as the pair whirled to face him; he got in the first shot.

But it wasn't the last. The quiet street exploded with gun-fire, the lances of reddish flame splitting the gloom. A slug ripped the crown of his hat. A second glanced off his cart-ridge belt and hurled him sideways with the shock. He caught his balance, fired again and again. Then he lowered his smoking Colts and peered through the powder fog at the two motionless forms sprawled in the dust.

Questioning shouts were sounding, not far off. He bounded forward, took a quick look at the dead faces, whirled and raced along the street at top speed for the shouts were draw-ing nearer. He whisked around a corner with unabated speed, turning another, and a third and slowed his pace. Directly ahead was the well lighted business section. A few moments more and he entered a *cantina* where he was known and took a table. A waiter, bowing and smiling, took his order. Slade relaxed in his chair and waited.

He didn't have long to wait. Before ten minutes had passed,

two excited Mexicans entered and were immediately the center of a crowd of patrons. Slade, listening intently, was able to catch fragments of what was said.

"Dead! Of bullet wounds! They wore the robes of the brothers! But they were not brothers! They were *Americanos!* Why did they fight and kill? No one knows! Why did they wear the robe of the brothers? No one knows! It was sacrilege! But *El Dios* is just! Retribution was swift!"

Slade felt that whether or not it was sacrilege was a matter of personal conviction; but he also felt it was about the most original disguise he had ever known to be adopted by a pair of owlhoots.

Only his meticulous noting of details, no matter how small, and his instant evaluation of their possible meaning, had saved him. The robes were somewhat short on the tall men, and beneath them he had seen, not the sandals universally worn by the brothers, but *rangeland riding boots!*

Listening to the babble of conversation, he gathered that the general conclusion was that the two men had slain each other. Which was all to the good so far as he was concerned.

Yes, Juan Covelo was a man to reckon with, all right. He was convinced that neither of the dead attackers was Covelo. Both were tall men and his quick glance had told him that their coloring was light, as were their eyes.

The *cantina* owner, fat and jolly, appeared bearing a bottle that Slade knew contained his choicest vintage. Behind him came a waiter with crystal goblets.

The proprietor seated himself as the waiter opened the bottle with a flourish. Not until the goblets were rimmed with the ruby wine did the owner speak, raising his glass in salute. "It is good to see you again, *Cápitan.*"

"And it is good to see you again, Miguel," Slade replied, also raising his glass. They drank together. The waiter instantly refilled the glasses and moved away. Miguel twinkled his shrewd little eyes at Slade.

"We have with us the excitement," he observed. "But where is *El Halcón* is always excitement, and—justice!"

"Thank you, Miguel, I'm glad you think so," Slade answered.

"Miguel does not think, Miguel *knows*," was the instant rejoinder. "Did the *ladrones* attempt to kill you?"

"They did," Slade replied. Briefly, he outlined what happened and how he had penetrated the disguise in the nick of time. Miguel shook his head in admiration.

"The eyes of *El Halcón* see all," he stated. "Why did they seek to kill you, *Cápitan?*"

Slade countered with a question of his own. "Ever hear of Juan Covelo?" he asked.

"A man most evil," Miguel answered. "Of his deeds I have heard."

"Any notion who he might be?"

Miguel shook his head and replied in the poetic metaphor of *Mejico*, "He is a shadow. A shadow that weaves in and out amid the shadows like a spirit of evil transplanted from another age. Without mercy, without conscience. A man who has sold his soul to the Devil and is one with the Lord of Ill."

"Like unto the Unjust Judge of the Scriptures," Slade commented. "He fears not God neither regardeth he man."

"Precisely," said Miguel. "Of him this I have learned that I believe to be true. That he abides in El Paso, where he plans his baleful deeds. His thoughts are wicked, his acts worse. You seek him, *Cápitan?*"

"I do," Slade answered. Miguel again shook his head.

"If any other than *El Halcón,* the just, the good, the able had said it, I would say that one had taken leave of the senses *El Dios* gave him," he declared. "But if *El Halcón* seeks, he will find, and Covelo will find the justice long overdue. And those two *ladrones* were members of his band?"

"So I presume," Slade replied.

"And *their* sins found them out," Miguel commented grimly. "So in the end will it be with Juan Covelo," he added with conviction.

"I hope you're right," Slade said cheerfully.

"I am," Miguel stated as one who defies contradiction. "*Cápitan* will pardon? My bartender beckons."

"Care for all *El Cápitan*'s wants," he told the waiter, who at once approached the table.

"I think it's about time I had something to eat," Slade said. The waiter smiled broadly.

"Already the food prepares, *Don* Miguel's orders," he replied.

"*Don* Miguel anticipates," Slade chuckled.

"Ha! he eats," said the waiter. "He knows when the food is good."

Slade enjoyed a really excellent meal, Miguel's *cantina* being famous for its cuisine. After which he smoked a cigarette over a final cup of coffee and reviewed recent events, not without a certain satisfaction.

He hadn't learned much from Miguel other than substantiation of his own opinion that Covelo had his real headquarters in El Paso, although Slade thought it highly likely that he had a hidden hole-up somewhere else. That plus a vote of confidence from the *cantina* owner, which didn't hurt.

Also, Covelo had to date lost at least eight of his following, which would not tend to promote unity in the organization. Very likely at the moment there was angry speculation as to why and how the attempt on his life had failed so signally. Covelo might well be forced to make the next try in person, his companions possibly displaying a certain reluctance to embark on the venture.

That possiblity Slade viewed with equanimity, affording as it would a chance for the showdown between the outlaw leader and himself.

However, he was not overly hopeful that such an eventuality would occur in the near future. Covelo undoubtedly had a firm grip on his following and his orders were apt to be obeyed without question, even though the chore might not be to their liking. Just the same, it was highly probable that *Señor* Covelo was doing some hard thinking about now.

So, everything considered, matters weren't going too bad. He relaxed comfortably and watched the dancers. He also watched the door, as was his custom. A moment later he saw a man enter who looked familiar. As the newcomer turned, the light from one of the hanging lamps fell full on his face and Slade recognized Gus Hansen, the owner of the Lemming Inn on Santa Fe Street in El Paso.

Hansen glanced around the room, his eye met Slade's and he waved his hand; Slade acknowledged the courtesy. Hansen walked to the far end of the bar, where Miguel greeted him cordially. For some time the pair conversed, having drinks together. Then Hansen departed, again waving to Slade. Miguel waddled over to the table.

"A nice *hombre*, the *Señor*," he remarked, sitting down and jerking his head toward the door. "With the frequency he drops in. He mentioned seeing you in his establishment earlier in the evening and asked your name. Keeps a sharp eye out for new business. I think he would like to open a *cantina* here in Juarez; he asks many questions relative to the business."

"I've a notion he could do worse," Slade commented. "In my opinion, Juarez is an up and coming pueblo. People to the north are beginning to realize more and more its possibilities as an entertainment center. Hansen would be wise to get in on the ground floor."

"So I advised him," Miguel admitted. "As you say, business is steadily growing and there will be plenty for all. Indeed I fear that soon the town will be too busy and crowded."

His shrewd little eyes seemed to look off into the far distances as he spoke and Slade suppressed a smile. Miguel was no longer young, but he still had itchy feet and was imbued with the pioneer spirit that sent his ancestors in their clanking armor forging into an unknown land, a savage wilderness, elaborately explaining that they sought treasure and conquest for their king. Not mentioning the lure of the ever advancing horizon, the soundless voices "calling!" the whispers in the night—"Something lost behind the ranges. Lost and waiting for you. Go!"

Slade glanced at the clock over the bar. "It's late," he said. "I think I'll mosey across the river and to bed."

"*Cápitan*," suggested Miguel, "why not sleep at my *casa* tonight? You have slept there before. It *is* late, and it's a long walk back to El Paso, and that bridge is dark and lonely at this time of night. My *criado* will joy to see you; he never sleeps till I come home. I'll be along later, after I close up."

"That's a notion," Slade admitted. "I don't feel like that long walk tonight. Okay, see you in the morning."

It was but a short distance to Miguel's house, where the old servant welcomed him warmly and conducted him to a comfortable room. He slept soundly till midmorning, awakening to find a bountiful breakfast awaiting him.

"The *patron* still sleeps," said the *criado*. "He will not arise for an hour."

Slade took his ease in the living room over coffee and cigarettes, and waited. After a while Miguel put in an appearance, hiding a yawn behind a plump hand. He sat down and accepted the cigarette Slade rolled for him.

"Did not I say that bridge is bad at night?" he remarked. "Last night, shortly after you left the *cantina*, a man was murdered on the south approach, shot in the back."

7 . . .

"The devil you say!" Slade exclaimed. "Somebody you knew?"

"No, I knew him not," replied Miguel. "He was an *Americano*, a cowboy I would say from his clothes."

"Wonder why he was killed?" Slade said. "Robbery?"

"I think not," answered Miguel. "There was money in his pockets, and he carried a gold watch. An *amigo* of mine was close by when the shooting occurred, several shots. He did not see the shooting, but he heard. Discreetly, he did not at once go to investigate but reported to the *jefe politico*, the chief of police."

Miguel glanced around and instinctively lowered his voice. "He told me, when he did not tell others, that right after the shooting he heard a cry, '*Buenas noches, Señor!*'"

Slade whistled under his breath. "Looks like Covelo struck again," he remarked. "Or one of his imitators." Miguel nodded sober agreement.

"Would you like to view the body?" he asked. "Perhaps you might recognize him. The *alcalde* is endeavoring to learn his name."

"Yes, I think I would," Slade replied.

After Miguel had breakfasted, they repaired to the mayor's office. The *alcalde* himself escorted them to the undertaking establishment where the body was laid out. A single glance told Slade he had never before seen the man.

In life he had been a tall man, something over six feet, and broad shouldered, his age somewhere around thirty, Slade estimated. His complexion and his hair were dark, his eyes blue.

After examining the dead hands, Slade announced, "He had been a cowhand, all right, but had not worked at it recently."

"Doubtless a wanderer," said the *alcalde*. "We get many such here."

43

"When I reach El Paso, I'll mention the matter to Sheriff Hart," Slade promised. "The chances are the fellow left a horse somewhere, and if the sheriff can locate it, there's a possibility that it might afford a clue to his identity."

"*Gracias*," said the mayor. "That I will appreciate."

As they headed for the *cantina,* Miguel asked, "Well, what do you think?"

"I think," Slade replied, "that he was the unfortunate victim of mistaken identity."

Sí?"

"Yes. The man was close to my height and of somewhat similar build, and his features would have been indistinguishable in the semi-dark of the approach. I would say that the killers watched me leave the *cantina* and walk in the general direction of the bridge. They hurried ahead, concealed themselves and waited. Then that poor devil came along at just the wrong time, for him."

Miguel swore in two languages, with a few pungent Yaqui expletives thrown in for good measure.

"And had you attempted to cross the bridge, *you* would have been killed," he concluded.

"Possibly," Slade conceded, not bothering to point out that drygulching *El Halcón* would have been a somewhat different proposition from gunning down an unsuspecting stranger who had no reason to anticipate harm.

Miguel was silent a moment, then, "Does not the '*Buenas noches, Señor!*' that was called seem to indicate that Covelo himself was one of the *ladrones*?" he asked.

"Could be, but not necessarily so," Slade replied. "That possibility must be considered as important, though; it might provide a clue to Covelo's identity. Just how, I don't at the moment see, but I'm not overlooking it. Yes, Covelo may have made a bad mistake there. Well, anyhow, another count against Covelo."

Regarding the granite lines of Slade's face and the look in his icy eyes, Miguel felt devoutly thankful that *he* was not in Juan Covelo's position.

Suddenly Slade chuckled, the devils of laughter leaping to the front of his eyes.

"Now what?" asked Miguel. "I don't see anything funny about it."

"I was thinking how surprised Covelo will be when he sets eyes on me," Slade explained. "He'll be ready to contradict Swinburne."

"Swinburne?"

"Yes, the English poet who wrote, 'That dead men rise up never.' "

Miguel couldn't find anything in his mission taught English to properly express his feelings and resorted to weird Spanish cuss words he thought did justice to the occasion. Slade listened admiringly and stored some of the choicer vituperations in his memory against possible future need. He felt that never before had he the faintest conception of the breadth and depth of the objurgatory powers of an angry Mexican, for Miguel went on without stopping for a full three minutes and he scarcely ever repeated himself.

"Come!" he said at last, when he was forced to pause for breath, "the wine I need; my throat she hurt."

"I'd think it would be scorched," Slade commented.

In the *cantina*, the wine, Miguel's choice vintage, was quickly forthcoming and both felt the better therefor.

"By the way," Slade remarked, "the *alcalde* made no reference to the other two bodies that were picked up last night."

Miguel shrugged with Latin expressiveness. "Oh, that was considered a matter of personal difference between the two and not worthy of comment, although there was some speculation as to why they wore the robes of brothers," he replied. "Now what?"

"Now," Slade said, "I'm going to mosey across the river for a talk with Sheriff Hart. I'll be seeing you, and thanks for everything."

"*Vaya usted con Dios! Hasta luego*. Go you with God! 'Til we meet again!" said Miguel.

Slade walked slowly up the slope of the bridge approach. Abruptly he paused and for some minutes stood studying the approach ahead with eyes that missed no detail. Finally he shook his head and walked on, his face thoughtful.

As Slade's account of the previous night's happenings progressed, Sheriff Hart's comments compared favorably with Miguel's.

"After you hot and heavy, eh?" he growled when the Ranger paused.

"Looks sort of that way," Slade conceded cheerfully. "Too hot and heavy for their own good, perhaps. Such impetuosity clouds the judgment and causes folks to do foolish things."

"Uh-huh, Covelo must be fit to be hogtied about now," agreed Hart. "Must have given him something of a jolt, after having things his own way for quite a spell. Lost eight of his hellions and a good part of the loot from his last raid. Yep,

I reckon he feels sort of put out. Looks like you've got him on the run."

"But not enough," Slade answered. "I still don't know who he is or where he hangs out. So far he's just a shadow."

"A darn solid shadow," grunted Hart. "Well, you've always been good at dropping a loop on shadows; don't see any reason why you should fail now.

"By the way," he added, "did you take a look at those two new places on Santa Fe Street I told you about?"

"Yes, I visited both," Slade replied.

"What do you think of them?"

"Nothing outstanding about either," Slade answered. "The Lemming Inn is the better furnished and equipped and I'd say the clientele is a shade above that of The Tank, which appears to cater mostly to rivermen and cowhands. In each was a sprinkling of the 'passing through' brand."

"Find them everywhere," growled Hart. "Did you get to see the owners?"

"Yes, I met both," Slade replied.

"What did you think of *them*?"

"Brian was talkative, Hansen was not, although pleasant enough. He dropped in at Miguel's *cantina* while I was there. Miguel thinks well of him."

" 'Pears to be all right, so far as I can judge," agreed the sheriff. "As I said before, I'm not so sure about Brian. Still looks more Mexican to me than Irish."

Slade smiled, but did not otherwise comment.

"And nobody knew that poor devil who was murdered on the bridge?"

"So it would seem," Slade replied. "I think it would be a good idea for you to ride over there with me after we have something to eat. Just the bare chance that you might recognize him. He was a cowhand, all right, though as I mentioned to the *alcalde,* he had not worked at it recently, at least not enough to mark his hands. However, that doesn't necessarily mean that there was something off-color about him. May have just been a chuckline rider with only an odd job of setting posts, mending corral fences and cleaning up around the ranchhouse and barn now and then to keep him in tobacco and whiskey money. If you can locate his horse somewhere here in town, it might give us a line on him."

"Could be," the sheriff agreed. "I'll set a couple of the boys to combing the stables."

His call to the outer office brought a deputy who received his instructions and hurried out to search the various livery stables. Slade and Hart had a bite in the Lookout, then rode across the river and gave the body of the murdered cowboy a onceover.

However, they had their ride for nothing. Hart had never seen the man before, and so far nobody in Juarez had come forward with a clue to his identity.

"Well, guess we might as well head back to the office and see if Bob has managed to learn anything relative to that horse," Slade decided.

Once again, as they breasted the slope of the approach, Slade halted, the sheriff drawing rein beside him, and once again he studied his surroundings. Hart looked a question.

"I think," Slade said slowly, "that I made a mistake."

"A mistake?"

"Yes, if Covelo is anything like as smart as he is supposed to be and knows *El Halcón*'s habits as he is supposed to know them."

"What in blazes are you getting at, anyhow?" Hart exclaimed exasperatedly. "How did you make a mistake?"

"In jumping to the conclusion that the killing here on the bridge last night was a case of mistaken identity, that the killers thought they were gunning me," Slade explained.

"I still don't get it," said Hart. "Make it clear, will you, please."

"Directly ahead is where the body was found," Slade replied. "Remember, the man was shot in the back, twice. The killer, or killers, which was more likely the case, must have stood in that shallow niche in the parapet which protects the edge of the approach. The victim must have passed right by them, either without seeing them, or recognizing them as persons he had, or thought he had, no reason to fear. In other words, a very clumsily set trap that would have been instantly spotted by someone accustomed to keeping a watch on his surroundings."

"Uh-huh, I'm getting it," said Hart. "The sort of a trap *El Halcón* would never have gotten caught in."

"Precisely," Slade agreed. "Does it look reasonable that an individual of Covelo's undoubted intelligence would have engineered so stupid a performance?"

"No, it don't," growled Hart. "I'd say they got the jigger they were after. But why the devil was he killed?"

"As to that I haven't the slightest notion, yet," Slade replied. "Come on; let's see what Bob has to say about the horse."

8 . . .

Bob, the deputy, was not present when they arrived at the office, but a few minutes later he came hurrying in.

"Yep, I found it," he answered the sheriff's question. "Over at old Si Jasper's livery stable. Si said a feller left it there early yesterday morning. Said he had begun wondering why the feller didn't show up to claim it—had told Si he'd be needing it early this morning. The description you gave me of the dead jigger fitted that feller to a T, or so Si said."

The deputy paused to roll a cigarette. Slade waited expectantly, for he sensed he had more to say.

"Something funny about that horse," Bob resumed. "Just a little while before I got there, Si said, a coupla jiggers showed up and wanted to take out the horse and the rig. Si wouldn't let them. Told them that only the man who brought a horse into his stable could take it out. Jiggers seemed in the notion of arg'fyin' the point and one of 'em sorta dropped his hand to the iron he was packing."

Bob paused to puff hard on his cigarette. "Yes?" prompted the sheriff.

"Uh-huh," said Bob, "and the next thing those two gents knew they were lookin' into the muzzles of that six-gauge shotgun Si always keeps handy. Si told them to get the blankety-blank-blank outa there, pronto."

"What did they do?" asked Hart.

"They got," Bob replied laconically. "Can't say as I blame 'em. Them six-gauge muzzles musta looked about the size of nail kegs, and I've a notion old Si didn't look over friendly. Sort of a cantankerous gent at all times, to say nothing of when he's put out about something; then he could give a teased Gila monster cards and spades."

The sheriff swore with whole-hearted fervor. "What in the blinkin' blue blazes?" he demanded of nobody in particular.

Slade stood up. "Come on," he said. "I want to have a look

at that horse, and the rig; I'm getting a notion. Bob, you stay here in case we want you in a hurry."

"Okay," replied the deputy, settling himself comfortably in his chair.

It was but a short walk to the livery stable. Slade and old Si Jasper were introduced and shook hands.

"First the horse," Slade said. Jasper designated the animal.

"A darn good looking cayuse," commented the sheriff.

"Yes, a fine horse," Slade agreed. "Has plenty of speed, I'd say, which is all to the good. Now I want to see the saddle pouches."

Jasper procured them. Slade thrust in a hand to draw forth a pair of overalls, a shirt, and several pairs of socks.

"Just duds, eh?" remarked Hart. "Reckon that's all."

"Not quite," Slade replied as his groping hand struck something hard. "Just as I thought. This pouch has a false lining; here's a barely noticeable slit at the top."

He worked his hand into the slit and drew forth roll after roll of wrapped coins. Ripping one of the wrappers revealed a yellow gleam.

"Holy hoptoads!" barked the sheriff. "Double-sawbuck yellow boys! Why there must be a thousand dollars there."

"And a little more," Slade said, turning one of the twenty-dollar gold pieces over in his fingers.

"But where in blazes did it come from? What was that hellion doing with all that money?" demanded the bewildered peace officer. Old Si joined in with a few pungent remarks of his own.

"Part of the stage coach holdup loot, of course," Slade explained. "Another example of the fact that there's very little honor among thieves. The hellion was holding out on the bunch. Covelo caught on somehow and had him executed as a warning to others, then sent a couple of his sidewinders to tie onto the horse and the loot. This may work to our advantage."

He leaned against the stall, rolled a cigarette and for some moments stood lost in thought.

"Arch," he said at length to the sheriff, "that newcomer to the section who was one of your specials the other night when we had the shindig with Covelo and his bunch—I imagine it is not generally known he is connected with your office?"

"That's right," replied Hart. "Was the first time he'd worked with me. Name's Porter, Newt Porter. He used to be a deputy sheriff over in Brewster County. My brother Rance, who's sheriff of Hudspeth County, knew him well, and when Porter

decided to move over this way and take a job he'd been offered, Rance gave him a letter to me. Said he'd be a good man
to tie onto whenever I happened to need a hand."

Slade nodded. "Think you could round him up in a hurry?"

"Sure; I know where he'll be about this time of day," Hart
answered. "He's taking it easy for a few days before going to
work."

"Fine!" Slade said. He turned to Jasper. "Si," he said,
"Porter will come for the horse and the rig at just about
sundown; he'll bring a note from the sheriff introducing him.
Let him have them."

"Certain," agreed Jasper.

"Okay," Slade said. "Pocket that *dinero*, Arch, and let's go.
Be seeing you, Si. We'll have Bob bring Porter in the back
way, Arch."

At the office, Bob, the deputy, was at once dispatched to
round up Newt Porter. Very shortly he returned with the
special in tow. Tersely, Slade explained the situation and un-
folded his plan.

"You will take the horse from the stable at sundown," he
told Porter. "Ride east as if you are heading for the Hueco
Mountains. I'm convinced that the men who tried to get the
horse and the rig this afternoon will be keeping tabs on the
stable, perhaps planning to make a try for the rig tonight.
They'll see you riding away from town and will follow you.
You should have no trouble keeping ahead of them on that
horse. Besides, it is hardly likely they'll try to close in on you
before you reach the brush country over to the east. Then
they will. Sheriff Hart and I are riding at once. Highly unlikely
that anybody will take note of our departure. Where the trail
runs into the brush we'll hole up and wait for you. From
there we should be able to scan the back trail for some distance. We'll spot you coming and, I expect, the pair that will
be tailing you. Then, if we have good luck, we'll drop a loop
on the hellions. If we can manage to take them alive, we may
learn something that will give us a line on Covelo himself. Understand?"

Porter took deliberate aim and drowned a fly perched on
the edge of a spittoon seven feet away.

"I do," he said, watching the fly frantically endeavoring
to swim out of the flood of tobacco juice. He gazed at Slade
in wordless admiration. So did Sheriff Hart.

Another example of *El Halcón*'s unique ability to put himself in the place of the outlaws, to think as they would think,
to plan as they would plan.

Confident that Porter would handle the chore properly, Slade and the sheriff hurried to secure their horses. Once clear of the town, they rode east at a fast pace.

"There'll be a bright moon a couple of hours after sunset," Slade remarked. "That should simplify matters for us. I feel sure the devils will come to our lure. Well, we'll see."

"Sounds good to me," Hart commented. "May give us a real break."

"I hope so," Slade replied. "We need one. If that hellion is allowed to run around loose much longer there'll be more killings of innocent people; he's in the nature of a mad dog."

A couple of miles out of town, Slade drew rein on the crest of a low rise and for several minutes gazed back the way they had come.

"Well, appears we are not wearing a tail," he said. "I really believe it is going to work out." They rode on, the wall of the Huecos steadily drawing nearer, with a long stretch of brush land running to their precipitous slopes.

The sun sank in chromatic splendor. The western sky blazed scarlet and gold that merged with the pale mauve in the east. The crests of the Huecos were ringed about with saffron flame, their mighty shoulders swathed in royal purple. Everywhere was the quiet beauty of the dying year as the day sank to rest and gave place to the ebon robe of night sown and spangled with the silver of the blossoming stars.

A fair land, Slade thought. Well worth fighting for. A privilege to battle the powers of lust and greed to maintain its pristine purity so that decent folks can live and prosper, taking their honest share of the good it so bountifully offered to all.

Which was the reason why Walt Slade was a Texas Ranger instead of holding a much more remunerative position with some great industrial concern.

Shortly before the death of his father, which followed business reverses that occasioned the loss of the elder Slade's ranch, young Walt had graduated from a famous college of engineering. His intention had been to take a postgraduate course in special subjects to round out his education and better fit him for the profession he planned to make his life work.

This, however, became impossible at the time. While trying to make up his mind just what course to follow, he received a suggestion from Captain Jim McNelty, the famous Commander of the Border Battalion of the Texas Rangers.

"Walt," said Captain Jim, "you have worked with me some during summer vacations and seemed to like the work, and you are certainly excellent Ranger material. So why not come into the Rangers for a while and pursue your studies during spare time. What do you say?"

After thinking it over, Slade decided the notion was a good one and signed up with Captain Jim. Long since he had gotten more from private study than he could have hoped to acquire from the postgrad course and was eminently fitted to take up the profession of engineering. Already he had received attractive offers from influential people he had contacted in the course of his Ranger activities, and more than once his knowledge of engineering had come in mighty handy.

But meanwhile, Ranger work had gotten a strong hold on him, providing as it did so many opportunities to do good and to help deserving people, and he was loath to sever connections with the famous body of law enforcement officers. He was young; plenty of time to be an engineer. He'd stick with the Rangers for a while.

So as he and Sheriff Hart rode toward the frowning loom of the Huecos shouldering the sky, Walt Slade felt uplifted. Here again was opportunity to serve the land he loved.

9 . . .

The moon rose, flooding the prairie with brilliant light. Slade turned again to look back the way they had come.

"Perfect," he said. "The brush land begins less than a mile ahead, and in this light we can see the back trail for more than a mile from the edge of the growth."

They continued on their way, reaching the point where the open prairie ended and was replaced by a broad stand of chaparral into which the trail flowed.

Fifty yards or so from the west edge of the brush the trail curved sharply and beyond the apex of the curve the growth edged away from the track to form a small clearing bathed in the white flood of the moonlight. Slade drew rein.

"This is made to order for us," he exulted. "Here is where we will stop Porter. Now we'll slide the horses back into the growth and flip out the bits so they can graze. Shadow won't stray and I imagine your critter won't either."

"That's right, he's well-trained," said Hart. Slade nodded and turned Shadow's nose to the north. A short distance of threading their way through the chaparral and they came to another and smaller open space where there was a scanty growth of grass.

"Now what?" Hart asked after the horses were cared for.

"Now back to the edge of the brush and keep watch," Slade replied. "I'm afraid we'll have quite a wait, so we'll make ourselves comfortable. A smoke won't go bad about now and we don't have to worry about giving ourselves away; we'll get ample warning of anybody coming along."

It did prove to be a long wait. An hour passed slowly, a second even more slowly and the dragging minutes of a third jogged along. And still the back trail stretched lonely and deserted with no sign of life even the keen eyes of *El Halcón* could discern.

"Wonder if there was a slip-up of some kind," worried the

sheriff. "I sure hope nothing bad's happened to Porter."

"There hasn't, so far," Slade replied, his eyes fixed on the distant trail. "He's just showed, and he's splitting the wind, too."

The sheriff stared with squinted eyes. "Blast it! I can't see anything," he grumbled.

"You will in a minute," Slade assured him. "Keep your eyes on the trail."

Another moment or two and Hart uttered an exclamation, "I see him now. He is siftin' sand, all right."

"And with good reason," Slade said grimly. "Here come the two devils, and they're closing the distance. Must be mighty well mounted. They're trying to get him in range before he makes the brush, and I'm afraid they'll do it. This is getting too darn interesting for comfort. That horse evidently isn't as good as we thought he was. Has speed, all right, but he lacks endurance. And, blast it! I seem to get stupider as I grow older; we should have brought the rifles along. Six-guns are no good at that distance, and we haven't time to go back for them."

"What the devil are we going to do?" demanded the sheriff, hopping with excitement.

"We can only wait, and if it comes to a showdown try to create a diversion with our Colts," Slade said. "May not come to that, though; they're still more than six hundred yards to the rear, and that's a long distance for shooting from the back of a racing horse. There they go!"

His keen eyes had detected a flicker of pale flame where the pursuers urged their horses to greater speed. A moment later came the metallic clang of the distant rifle. Again and again. Porter was hunched low in his saddle, spurring his failing mount.

Tense, hardly breathing, they watched the grim race with death. Slade concentrated on the situation with an earnestness that amounted to mental agony, weighing Porter's chances of reaching the shelter of the brush before a lucky shot brought him down, against the advisability of opening up with their sixes in the hope of throwing the pursuit off balance. Porter was now little more than four hundred yards from the sanctuary of the growth, but the pursuers had closed the distance greatly. Slade estimated they were now less than three hundred yards to the rear of the fugitive. If they were shrewd enough to pull up and take deliberate aim, they could hardly fail to score a hit.

But they didn't. In the excitement of the chase they overlooked opportunity and came charging on at full speed, firing as they came. Slade arrived at a decision, praying that he wasn't making a mistake.

"Back to the clearing," he said. "When Porter shows, call to him to stop and leave his horse standing in the trail. You do the talking, he'll recognize your voice; he'll be expecting us to be somewhere close when he hits the brush."

"If he does," muttered Hart as they raced back down the trail and crouched in the growth at the edge of the clearing. Another moment and Slade's ears caught the beat of a horse's hoofs, a staggering beat, for the animal had just about reached the limit of his strength. But loud, loud was the booming of the rifles. Slade held his breath and tensed for instant action.

Abruptly the sound of the thudding irons changed a little. Slade gave an exultant exclamation. "He made it! He's in the brush! Stop him soon as he shows."

Around the bend shambled Porter's mount, lurching and reeling.

"Hold it, Newt!" called the sheriff. "Unfork and in here with us."

"Leave the horse where it is," Slade added.

Porter instantly obeyed, swinging from the saddle and diving into the brush alongside Slade and the sheriff. The exhausted horse stood right where it was, front legs wide spread, head hanging.

Again the loudening beat of hoofs. Again the slight change of sound.

"Get set!" Slade whispered. "Here they come."

Around the bend careened the pursuers. The riders spotted the standing horse and jerked their mounts to a slithering halt, storming exclamations.

"Look out!" one shouted. "He's holed up!"

Slade's great voice rolled in thunder, "Elevate! You're covered!"

The two outlaws jumped in their saddles, mouthing curses. Slowly their hands raised shoulder high. Slade and the others stepped into view.

Slade saw a hand dart forward. He drew and shot the instant before the sleeve gun spat flame. The derringer slug fanned his face, but the gunman gave a bubbling shriek and toppled from the hull. Hart and Porter opened fire, shooting as fast as they could pull trigger.

"Hold it! Hold it!" Slade shouted as the second rider reeled and fell. His gun ready for instant action, he glided forward, his eyes never leaving the two forms sprawled in the dust. But to his bitter disappointment both were dead, the first with a bullet slashed throat, the second shot to pieces.

"Well, didn't work out as well as we'd hoped it would, but it could have been worse," he said as he ejected the spent shell from his gun and replaced it with a fresh cartridge.

"Yep, not too bad," agreed the sheriff. "Two more of the sidewinders accounted for, and a sizeable chunk of the stage coach loot recovered. And," he added impressively, "if you hadn't spotted that infernal sleeve gun like you did, it could have been a helluva sight worse; one of us would very likely have gotten it. How'd you catch onto what the hellion had in mind?"

"I learned long ago to watch out for just such a move," Slade explained. "When a man raises his hands slowly, keep an eye on them. That fellow raised his left hand straight up, in the natural position, but the right was jutting to the front, out of line with the other, and *that* was the natural position for sliding a gun out of the sleeve into the palm of his hand. Takes practice to master it, but it's a fast and deadly draw when it is mastered, and sometimes catches a man off guard."

"Uh-huh, but not *El Halcón*," Hart observed dryly. Slade turned to Porter.

"Newt, you sure handled your chore properly," he complimented the special.

"But when that cayuse began getting groggy I began wondering a mite if I'd be able to go through with it and stay in one piece," Porter chuckled. "Hearing you fellers yelp made me feel mighty good."

Slade's first thought was for Porter's exhausted horse. He gave the animal a good rubdown, flipped out the bit and poured water from his canteen into cupped hands for it to drink. It greedily drank the entire contents of the canteen and asked for more.

"That'll be enough for now," Slade told it. "Too much and you'll be sick. You can have another good swig when we reach that creek a couple of miles to the west. Come on, now, and surround some grass."

He led the cayuse to where Shadow and the sheriff's mount were cropping and returned to his companions, after repeating the performance with the outlaws' horses, which had also been too winded to run more than a few yards down the trail and were easily caught.

In the meanwhile, the sheriff had been examining the dead men and emptying their pockets.

"Ornery looking scuts," he observed.

"About average, I'd say," Slade replied, peering at the dead faces.

"Look what I took off the yellow haired one," said the sheriff, handing Slade a round flat tin box. "Funny thing for a cowhand to be packing around."

Slade pried off the lid to reveal a fine brownish powder.

"Copenhagen snuff," he announced. "Yes, rather unusual for a cowhand to have it in his possession. Favored by seamen, especially the Scandinavians." He turned to the dead man again.

"Fellow does have a Norse look," he commented. He examined the man's hands with care.

"Has worked as a cowhand, but not for a long time," was his verdict. "I'd say from certain marks on his fingers that he had recently been a seaman. Interesting." He slipped the box into his pocket. "Anything else?" he asked.

"Nothing out of the ordinary, except quite a passel of *dinero*," answered Hart.

"I've a notion Porter can use it to put back some of the weight he lost in the course of that ride," Slade suggested.

"You're darn right I can," said Porter as the sheriff passed him the money. "Figure I sweated off about twenty pounds when those hellions were closing in on me. Was beginning to figure my cook was goosed—I mean my coose was—oh, the devil! Just forget all about it. What shall we do with the carcasses?"

"Pack them to town, after the horses have rested a bit," Slade decided. "Arch can put them on exhibition. Maybe somebody will recognize them."

"Only barkeeps ever do and they can't remember anything that would do any good," grumbled the sheriff. "We'll make a try at it, though; something might work out. Now what?"

"Now we might as well make ourselves comfortable for an hour or so until the horses are fit to travel," Slade replied. "Luckily it's a nice night and not cold."

Seating themselves at the edge of the brush, with convenient trunks at their backs, they smoked and talked. Porter explained that he was little more than a mile out of town when he spotted the two outlaws on his trail.

"But for a while they didn't try to catch up," he said. "Then when they did start speeding, that cayuse I rode held his own without any trouble, for a while. Couldn't keep it up, though, and things didn't look so good."

"I imagine not," Slade agreed. "The odds were against you. But you did a bang-up chore of keeping ahead of them and leading them on. I think, Arch, that you'd better try and wean him away from that job with the Liston people and have him made a full-fledged deputy; he's a natural for a peace officer."

Hart nodded emphatic agreement and Porter looked very pleased.

After a while, Slade glanced at his watch and stood up. "Guess we might as well be ambling," he said. "The cayuses should be in good shape by now."

The horses were collected, the bodies roped to the saddles of the two spares. Sheriff Hart regarded them with grim satisfaction.

"Makes eleven altogether, I believe," he remarked. "At this rate *amigo* Covelo will soon find himself short a bunch. And if he gets what's coming to him, he'll end up with a long-stretched neck."

"Or a good dose of lead pizening, which I figure will be more likely," added Porter.

Travelling with the awkwardly burdened horses was slow and the false dawn was flitting ghost-like across the sky when they reached El Paso. The bodies were laid out in the sheriff's office and, after the horses were cared for, everybody tumbled into bed, too tired to even eat.

10 . . .

Walt Slade made up for that lack around noon, however, putting away a bountiful breakfast at the Lookout with the appetite and perfect digestion of youth. After which he repaired to the sheriff's office where he found Hart already on the job.

"Us old folks don't need as much sleep as you younkers," he explained. "I've been here two hours. Lots of folks dropped in to have a look at the carcasses, but the same old story—nobody admits knowin' 'em. Well, what do you say? Shall we mosey over to the bank and give the folks there a nice surprise?"

The bank officials were pleasantly surprised to receive an additional thousand dollars and more of the stage hold-up money.

"At this rate we'll soon be breaking even," chuckled the cashier. "When you going to bring in some more, Arch?"

"Ask Slade," replied Hart. "He's the jigger who's been tying onto it."

"There'll be a reward for the recovery," said the cashier. "Looks like it should go to Mr. Slade." Hart nodded agreement, but *El Halcón* smilingly shook his head.

"If those two guards who were killed in the course of the hold-up left dependents, I think it would be more fitting that any reward money go to them," he said.

The cashier regarded him with respect. "That is nice of you, Mr. Slade," he said. "I don't think anybody will object to that."

"I'd like to see somebody try it," growled the sheriff. "Be seeing you, John."

"And what's the next move?" he asked when they were outside the bank. "The inquest on those two varmints won't be held till five o'clock. Doc McChesney, the coroner, is tied up till then."

"I think I'll visit an old friend of mine, Pablo Montez, who runs the big *cantina* down on Seventh Street in the Mexican section, not far from the bridge."

"Montez is all right, I know him well," nodded Hart. He crinkled his eyes at Slade.

"He's got a little niece, Carmen, who handles his book work and takes a whirl on the dance-floor now and then; she's a mighty purty gal."

"If she isn't, she has sure changed a lot since I last saw her," Slade said smilingly.

The sheriff chuckled and waited for Slade to continue.

"Not much goes on along the border that Pablo doesn't hear about," Slade added reflectively. "He has ways of obtaining information and may be able to give me a valuable hint. I'll be seeing you at the inquest."

Pablo's place was commodious and airy. The equipment was excellent and the adequate illumination came from many wax candles that cast a mellow and soothing glow over the polished and gleaming furnishings. A really good orchestra played soft music and the dance-floor girls were young and pretty. Slade thought the *cantina* was one of the nicest places in town. It was usually quiet and peaceful, although it could be turbulent at times. However, Pablo and his "young men," as he called them, had little trouble maintaining order.

Heads turned as Slade entered. Pablo himself, big, jolly and smiling, hurried to greet him with outstretched hand.

"*Cápitan!*" he exclaimed. "Wonderful it is to have you with us again. My young men heard you were in town and we have been awaiting you. Come! there is one who will joy to see you."

He led the way to the back room, closing the door behind them. Seated at a table covered with books and papers was a rather small girl with great dark eyes, curly dark hair, very red lips, an exquisitely proportioned figure and a roguish smile. She came to her feet with a glad cry and fairly hurled herself into Slade's arms.

"So you did come back!" she exclaimed.

"I did," Slade voiced the obvious. "Didn't I tell you I would?"

"Yes, but I didn't believe you. I figured some other woman had you roped and tied by now."

"I slipped out of the loop," he answered blithely. "How is everything?"

"Wonderful—now."

"Still live in the pretty little house on Kansas Street, that your father left you?"

"Yes."

"Still alone?"

"Yes, darn it! Still alone, with—memories."

"Memories sometimes translate into realities of the present," he pointed out.

"I hope so," she replied, smiling and blushing.

"I must check the bar," said Pablo, slipping out and closing the door.

"He checked it ten minutes ago," Carmen giggled. "Oh!"

It took Pablo quite a while to "check the bar." He even tapped lightly before entering.

"And now," he said, smiling benignly, "doubtless *Cápitan* desires to talk."

"Yes, and to ask some questions," Slade said. Pablo looked expectant.

"First, what do you know, if anything, about Juan Covelo?"

"One who has lived too long," Pablo answered instantly. Slade nodded.

"As to that, we agree," he said. "Now let's see if we agree on something else."

He produced the note that was slipped under the door of Sheriff Hart's office and laid it on the table. Carmen's breath caught in her throat. Pablo muttered an oath.

"Would you say this was written by a mission-taught Mexican?" Slade asked. Pablo shook his head.

"I do not think so," he replied. "One taught English by the *padres* would be unlikely to employ the word 'catch.' He would be much more apt to write 'capture.' "

Slade nodded. "But from the wording and the punctuation, would not one be inclined to believe that the writer was a man of some education?"

"Sí."

"Doubtless an *Americano*?"

"So I would assume," answered Pablo.

"So we agree on all points," Slade said. "I wished to know if you would corroborate my own beliefs. I'm glad you do, for it gives me something to work on."

"You are on the trail of that *ladrone*?"

"Yes."

Carmen sighed, and shuddered.

"Maybe I'll learn to take it," she said. "Guess I'll have to."

"Worry not, *caro mio*," Pablo said gently. "Remember, *El Halcón*, the good, the just, the compassionate, walks in the shadow of God's hand."

Carmen bowed her shapely head, and her lips moved as if in prayer.

"Thank you, Pablo," Slade said. "Have you any idea who Juan Covelo might be? I'm sure Covelo is not his real name, and I've a notion his headquarters are right here in El Paso."

"Both assumptions, I think, are correct," nodded Pablo. "It is difficult to persuade people to speak of such matters, for his name is a name of terror, but I have heard that a whisper says that somewhere here on the riverfront Covelo sits like a spider in its web and plots his wickedness." Slade nodded thoughtfully.

"I have something of the same notion," he said. "If so, it narrows the search a bit."

"My young men will peer and pry and listen," promised Pablo. "Up to the present, I gave the *ladrone* little thought, but now it is different. All will combine to assist *El Halcón*. And now, let us partake of food and drink. Come, Carmen, the work can wait; it must defer to the honored guest. While we dine, *Cápitan* will tell us of his adventures."

"And his conquests," laughed Carmen.

Slade enjoyed a really excellent dinner, for the cook outdid himself in honor of *El Halcón*. During the meal, quite a few of the patrons came over to greet him, including several of Pablo's young men whom he knew well. Which was gratifying, for these smiling, alert young Mexicans, artists with gun and knife, were valuable allies, which they had previously proven conclusively.

After a final cup of coffee and a cigarette, he glanced at the clock.

"Will have to get uptown for the inquest," he told his table companions, "but I'll be back later."

"You'd better be or I'll come looking for you," Carmen said ominously.

"I could think of worse fates," Slade smiled.

"Have a care," warned Pablo. "When a woman goes looking for a man it behooves him to be wary."

"I'll keep that in mind," Slade returned. "Just a question or two more before I go. What do you think of Joe Brian who owns The Tank over on Santa Fe Street?"

"A good businessman but not overly sociable," Pablo answered. "He impresses me as a man who has had to fight hard to get where he is and who looks on everyone as a possible adversary."

Slade nodded. "And Gus Hansen who runs the Lemming Inn?"

"Affable, courteous and, I would say, very shrewd. All men count with him, but none too much. I would say he has few confidants, if any; sufficient unto himself."

"Thank you," Slade said, and meant it. For he knew that shrewd old Pablo was an excellent judge of men and made a practice of studying his competitors.

He was glad that his own diagnosis of the two saloon-keepers tallied very well with Pablo's and he left the *cantina* in a thoughtful mood.

The inquest was a replica of those that went before. Plant 'em and forget 'em. And go get some more.

"And now," Slade told Sheriff Hart, "I aim to prowl the town a bit and see if I can spot somebody who appears to be a likely prospect. So far I haven't had much luck."

"No luck?"

"I wouldn't say that," Slade returned thoughtfully. "Somehow I have a vague notion, with nothing concrete on which to base it."

"One of your hunches, eh?"

"You might call it that," Slade admitted.

"Well, they usually work out."

"Sometimes," Slade replied. "By the way, where was Joe Brian located before he came here?"

"Around Tombstone, Arizona, I believe he said. Claims to be Texas born, though—Jeff Davis County. He mentioned quite a few folks over around Tombstone that he knew. Sheriff Behan, Billy Breckenridge, and Richard Gird, among others. The way he tells it, he did Gird something of a favor once, and Gird advanced the money to set him up in business here."

"That sounds like Gird, all right," Slade commented. "He's exceedingly wealthy and he does such things. Behan and Breckenridge are okay, too, and if Brian's handing out a straight line, he certainly has excellent connections."

"Uh-huh, if he's handin' out a straight line," the sheriff snorted. "A wonder he didn't include Wyatt Earp while he was at it."

"I imagine he was there some time after Wyatt and his brothers left Tombstone," Slade said. Hart grunted, and did not directly mention Brian again.

"Saw his neighbor, Gus Hansen, a little while ago," he remarked. "Dropped in for a look at the bodies just before you showed up. Said he thought he'd seen them around the river-front, but couldn't be sure. Said they got just what was coming to them; sounded like he meant it."

"Well, I'm heading for Pablo's *cantina* for a word with him and Carmen. Believe I'll stick around for a couple of days and rest up; feeling a mite tuckered."

"And no wonder," grunted Hart. "And then?"

"Then back to the Post. Captain Jim will very likely have something lined up for me by the time I get there."

Three days later Carmen, as she stroked Shadow's glossy neck, asked, "You'll be back?"

"I came back twice," he pointed out. "And they say the third time's the charm."

She laughed, although her eyes were wistful.

"I hope so," she said, and watched him, tall and graceful atop his great black horse, as he rode to where duty called and danger and new adventure waited.

11 . . .

At a leisurely pace, Slade covered the bustling town. Business was booming, everybody appeared satisfied with the present, optimistic as to the future. El Paso was a going concern, all right, with plenty of easy money floating around. This offered lucrative opportunities for gentlemen of the Juan Covelo brand.

He paused briefly at various places, studying faces, listening to scraps of conversation. But nowhere did he discover anything he considered of value. After a while he dropped in at the livery stable for a visit with Shadow.

"Horse," he told the big black, "maybe it's a sign that the brain is cracking up at last, but I'm evolving a theory, an outlandish theory that doesn't seem to make sense."

"Nothing new about that," Shadow's snort seemed to say.

"Maybe not," Slade conceded, "but this one is of a particularly loco variety. With mighty little on which to base it. Just a hooded cloak, a few words spoken by Sheriff Hart, and a box of Copenhagen snuff. Yes, utterly loco, but it won't down.

"Oh, sure, I know what you're thinking: 'Here we go again!' You've said that before, and sometimes you were wrong. So take it easy and don't be so darned pessimistic, and stop fussing. Maybe you'll get a chance to stretch your legs tomorrow. That'll put you in a better temper."

Shadow didn't argue the point and Slade departed. Gradually he worked his way toward the riverfront. Sunset flamed its splendor in the west and the lovely blue dusk sifted down from the mountain tops like impalpable dust. The lights of El Paso winked at those of Juarez across the river, and the lights of Juarez winked back, coyly.

It was well past dark when Slade found himself on Santa Fe Street. Here the town's boisterous night life was already in full swing with laughter and music, the clink of bottle necks against glass rims, the sprightly clang of gold pieces on the "mahogany," the flick of high heels on the dance-floors, and the cheerful hum of the roulette wheels as the little ball bounced from slot to slot. Slade felt his pulses quicken. He'd spend a little time here and then head for Pablo's *cantina* and Carmen; feminine companionship was in order.

He strolled on till he came to The Tank, which proved to be really hopping. The bar was crowded three deep, the games going full blast, the dance-floor jammed.

Slade was lucky enough to find a small vacant table close to the dance-floor from where he had a good view of the room and the swinging doors. The place was noisy and bois-terous but, at the moment at least, appeared harmless. The dance-floor girls weren't bad; neater and better looking than average, he thought. He studied the games for a while and decided that they were straight. Joe Brian evidently ran his establishment on the up-and-up, wisely realizing it would pay off in the end.

After a bit Brian, who had waved to him when he sat down, approached the table.

"Take a load off your feet," Slade invited. Brian did so and beckoned a waiter. He grinned, showing crooked but white and well cared for teeth.

"Well, here I am again, nosing in and trying to learn something about you, as you quickly guessed I was trying to do the other time you were here," he chuckled.

"Relative to the notorious *El Halcón*," Slade smiled, falling in with the other's humor. Brian shrugged derisively.

"The *El Halcón* yarn is just so much sheep dip," he said. "But I *have* got you placed Mr. Slade, to an extent, at least."

"Yes?"

"Yes. It came to me all of a sudden. Over in Tombstone one night, in the Oriental saloon, Wyatt Earp's old place, Johnny Behan and Dick Gird were discussing you. Seems Gird had received a letter from Wyatt Earp that day which recalled the matter to mind. Gird and Behan were telling some other fellers about how you backed down Curly Bill Brocius and John Ringo and once saved Wyatt Earp's life. They were very complimentary. Of course at that time your name didn't mean anything to me, and what they were talk-ing about happened before my time in Tombstone; but some-how the name stuck in my mind and, as I said, all of a sudden it came to me that you must have been the man they were talking about. Yes, they were very complimentary, and they both seem to think a lot of you."

"I've a notion the story grew considerably in the telling," Slade said.

"I doubt it," replied Brian. "Neither Behan nor Richard Gird are given to exaggeration. Anyhow, I consider I am honored in having you visit my establishment."

"Thank you, Mr. Brian," Slade said.

"I hope you'll like it here," Brian continued. "The boys get a mite rowdy at times, but it usually doesn't amount to much and I don't have much trouble quieting them down."

He grinned again and rose to his feet. "Talk about the devil, or something like that," he said with a chuckle. "Listen to that arg'fyin' down at the end of the bar. Getting louder by the second. Excuse me, please."

He hurried off to the scene of the disturbance. Slade watched his progress thoughtfully. He felt that Joe Brian was something of an enigma. He knew Tombstone, all right, and its citizens. Just how close was his contact with such men as Richard Gird remained to be learned. He had mentioned the silver tycoon in an offhand manner that hinted at familiarity. However, little men often claim association with big men even though the acquaintance is really but superficial. But somehow, Joe Brian didn't strike him as that sort. Rather, he seemed a man who stood on his own feet and didn't seek to bolster his self-confidence vicariously.

The speed with which the argument at the far end of the bar subsided appeared to strengthen the assumption; Joe Brian knew how and was able to handle his crowd.

All of which gave *El Halcón* food for thought. He wondered just how much Brian really did know. The answer to that might be of importance to himself. He finished his drink, waved goodnight to Brian and departed.

His next stop was the Lemming Inn, which was also crowded but less noisy. The waiter who served him in the course of his former visit, doubtless remembering a generous tip, hurried to meet him and escorted him to a table. Gus Hansen, at the far end of the bar, nodded cordially but did not immediately approach the table.

But Slade knew the owner was covertly studying him, apparently endeavoring to make up his mind to something. There was a speculative gleam in his dark blue eyes and he tapped nervously on the bar with the long fingers of his lean, muscular hand.

Why should his presence perturb Hansen? For Slade was confident it did. The answer to that question he was also anxious to discover. He shifted his attention to the dance-floor and the games. The girls were nice and had the look of square-shooters. The games were orderly, several undoubtedly for high stakes. And so far as Slade could see—and the eyes of *El Halcón* missed little—they were, like those at The Tank, conducted strictly on the level. So why should Hansen evince nervousness at the entrance of a comparative stranger? Another blasted unanswered question.

Of course his *El Halcón* reputation might have something to do with it. The presence of one whose antecedents were dubious, to say the least, could well give a bar owner grounds for concern. That *El Halcón* had enemies was an open secret and Hansen perhaps feared a corpse and cartridge session might get under way at any moment.

Oh, well, like Joe Brian, Hansen was something of an enigma and one more didn't matter particularly. The big "enigma" with whom he as a Texas Ranger had to contend was the elusive, mysterious, capable and ruthless Juan Covelo. And as to the identity of Covelo he had only a vague notion —playing a hunch.

Eventually Hansen did approach the table. He nodded pleasantly.

"Mr. Slade, is it not?" he stated rather than asked. "My friend Miguel Zaranda, over in Juarez, mentioned your name the other night. He regards you highly."

"Nice of him," Slade acknowledged.

Gus Hansen had a flashing smile when he chose to use it, although Slade felt it was tinged with a certain derisive quality as if Hansen were secretly amused at something.

"I have found Miguel's judgment of men highly dependable," he remarked.

"Thank you," Slade replied. "I hope you will not be disillusioned."

"I won't be, not in the least," Hansen said. Again the slightly derisive smile which Slade found disquieting. It seemed to hint that the saloonkeeper knew a lot more than he chose to divulge.

Hansen glanced around. "Busy night," he observed. "Payday nights always are. Enjoy yourself; I'll send over a drink." He strolled back to the end of the bar. A few moments later he disappeared into the back room and did not reappear.

Slade took his time with the drink Hansen sent over, sipping it, toying with the glass. Meanwhile he was scanning faces, listening to scraps of conversation, studying the Lemming Inn's varied patrons.

However, he discovered nothing he considered of importance. Hansen still did not reappear from the back room. So he tossed off the rest of his glass, said goodnight to the waiter and departed for Pablo's *cantina*.

He walked warily, as usual, but reached his *cantina* without experiencing any untoward incident, where he found Carmen awaiting him.

"I was beginning to think you weren't coming back," she said.

"Why not?"

"Lots of pretty girls in El Paso," she replied obliquely.

"But there can be but one superlative," he instantly countered.

Carmen laughed merrily. "I'm not going to give you the satisfaction of asking who is she," was her retort.

"No need to ask, just look," he answered, gesturing toward the bar mirror.

"That's similar to viewing a woman through the bottom of a whiskey glass," she said. "Look often enough and they all get beautiful."

"That's a notion," he agreed. "Waiter!"

"Just one," she said. "The cook is already preparing your dinner; he got busy the instant you came through the door and you must do justice to it or he will be desolated."

"If I don't, he must blame the distraction across the table," Slade answered. Carmen sniffed daintily.

"No woman can distract a hungry man from his food," she declared. "I'm going out to the kitchen to see how Felipe is coming along." She suited the action to the word.

Slade began manufacturing a cigarette, his gaze on the black square of a window directly across the room from where he sat, that opened onto an unlighted alley. Instinctively, as he talked with Carmen, he had watched that open window, just as he instinctively watched the swinging doors.

Suddenly he sensed movement beyond the square of blackness. But even as he tensed for instant action, from outside the window came a scream, a horrible bubbling scream, as if a man were shrieking with his throat full of blood.

Weaving and ducking, Slade bounded across the room. As he reached the window, his keen ears caught the patter of fast footsteps fading into the distance. He hesitated a moment, then peered out cautiously. On the ground directly beneath he could just make out a huddled something.

The *cantina* was in an uproar, everybody shouting at once,

yelling curses, bawling questions. Slade's great voice rolled through the tumult, "Pablo! Bring a light!"

A lamp was quickly forthcoming. Slade held it out the window, Pablo leaning beside him. The owner swore explosively.

The huddled something was the body of a man, his face resting in a pool of blood, which was not surprising since his head was very nearly severed from his body. In one stiffened hand he clutched a cocked gun.

12 . . .

Carmen was at Slade's side, her face paperwhite, her breast heaving.

"Are—are you all right?" she gasped.

"Just fine," he replied. "I wasn't out there."

"What happened?"

"Appears two gents had a difference of opinion and one used a knife before the other could use his gun," Slade equivocated.

Carmen shuddered. "That awful scream," she said. "It was terrible."

"Didn't sound very nice," Slade agreed. "Come away; what's outside isn't nice for you to look upon."

"I'm going back to the kitchen to lend Felipe a hand," she said. "Please stay in here."

"I will," he promised and turned to Pablo.

"Better send somebody to notify the sheriff and the town marshal," he told the owner. "And put somebody out there to keep an eye on that body till they arrive. Fortunately, it didn't happen in here."

Pablo shot him a keen look. "But too close for comfort," he growled. "I'll take care of everything." He hurried off to do so. Slade returned to his table, rolled his belated cigarette and waited.

He didn't have long to wait. A few minutes later a lithe young Mexican strolled in, glancing about. His features, his very dark complexion and his flashing black eyes denoted plenty of Yaqui blood. It was Gordo Allende, one of Pablo's young men, in whose company Slade had experienced an exciting adventure during the occasion of a former visit to El Paso. He gestured to a vacant chair.

Gordo approached the table and sat down, lowering his voice as he spoke.

"He was waiting," he said without preamble. "Crouched outside the window and waiting for Carmen to leave the table or change her position; she was right in line. When she

71

did leave, he straightened up and drew his gun. But my blade was swift, and sure. I think *Cápitan* understands."

Slade did understand, perfectly. He knew that from the moment he entered the *cantina*, Pablo's young men were keeping watch over him, and he shrewdly suspected that Gordo had been keeping an eye on him all evening. Gordo's next remark justified the surmise.

"The *ladrone* followed you when you left the Lemming Inn," he resumed. "He did not attempt to draw near, doubtless knowing nobody can approach *El Halcón* without being noted. When you entered the *cantina* he hesitated, then slipped into the alley. I followed *him*, and *Cápitan* knows that in the darkness I move as does the little shadow that loses itself at sunset. In the darkness I waited. I had thought my stroke would silence him at once, but it did not, so I departed from thence in the hurry."

"Thank you, Gordo," Slade said. "It was a nice try and had it not been for you, it might have succeeded."

"That is the doubtful," said Gordo. "*El Halcón* sees all. But why should I pass up the chance to rid the world of evil?" He grinned with a flash of white teeth, rose and sauntered to the bar. Slade shook his head. Gordo Allende was a good *amigo,* and able. But he was rather terrible.

Slade's dinner arrived, and Carmen with it. "But I'm afraid I can't eat a bite," she said. "I've still got the shakes." Nevertheless, she did pretty well.

"Now I feel like a new woman," she said, some little time later.

"The old one was good enough for me," Slade returned cheerfully. "Hello! Here comes the sheriff."

"And the town marshal," Carmen added.

After glancing inquiringly at Slade, who shook his head slightly, Hart engaged Pablo in conversation. A moment later they approached the table.

"Suppose we go out and have a look at the remains," the sheriff suggested. Carmen shuddered.

"Guess we could do worse," Slade agreed. Accompanied by Pablo and the marshal they made their way into the alley to where the body lay. A lamp was passed out the window. A wet bar rag was forthcoming, with which they wiped the blood from the dead face. A severe countenance with eyes that still stared in terror was revealed.

"About the same as the other hellions," Hart muttered. "Somebody sure took a swipe at him. If he sneezed, his head would fly off. Wonder who did it?"

"Hard to tell," replied Pablo. "Seems nobody saw it happen. There was a yell, and that was all."

The sheriff's lips twitched slightly, but he made no comment.

"Let's see what he's got on him," he said and began emptying the dead man's pockets, revealing nothing that Slade considered of significance. The stiffened fingers had to be pried from the gun butt.

"Good iron," observed Hart.

"Let's have a look at it," Slade said. He turned the weapon over in his slim fingers.

"A little unusual for this section," he remarked. "A forty-one calibre on a forty-five frame. Favored over in Arizona and California, but you seldom see one here.'

The sheriff's brows drew together, and again he glanced inquiringly at the Ranger who interpreted the glance.

"Quite a few folks from Arizona and California drift over this way," he observed pointedly. Hart grunted and let it go at that.

"I'll have the carcass packed off to the office," he said. "Reckon there's no sense in holding an inquest on this one; seems nobody saw what happened except the gent who handled the knife, and I've a notion he ain't talking. Let's go get a drink."

He dropped back to join Slade who had lingered for a moment.

"Well, what did happen?" he asked in an undertone.

Slade told him briefly. "It was a nice try, and if Gordo Allende didn't have cat feet and cat eyes in the dark, it might have worked. Of course what I saw was the hellion straightening up and drawing his gun, but one slip on my part would have meant curtains. However, Gordo took care of things with his usual efficiency."

"Gordo's all right," nodded the sheriff. "A good man to have for you; a bad one to have against you."

"You can say that double," Slade rejoined grimly. "Well, business doesn't appear to have been hurt much; things are booming."

"What's a killing more or less to these rum holes!" snorted the sheriff. "They thrive on 'em."

The *cantina* really was in a hilarious mood, noisier, more talkative than usual. Laughter and a babble of whirling words filled the air. Even the old sheriff and the elderly marshal appeared to catch a spark of the prevailing spirit, after a couple of snorts. Suddenly the former turned to Slade.

"What do you say, Walt, how about giving us a song?" he said. "Show 'em what the singingest man in the whole Southwest can do."

"Yes, *Cápitan*, please do," urged Pablo. Other voices joined in. Pablo beckoned the orchestra leader, who came forward, bobbing and grinning and bearing a guitar which he handed to Slade.

"Come, *Cápitan*," he pleaded.

"Well, it looks like I haven't much choice," Slade smiled. "I can stand it if you can."

The leader, strutting proudly, led the way to his little raised platform and bowed low to Slade, who turned to face a sea of expectant faces.

What did he sing? Just a homely little song of the range-land, such as men sing to drowsy cattle or around campfires lonely under the stars, but it was alchemized into a thing of beauty by the magic of a great voice. And as the golden, metallic baritone-base pealed and thundered through the room, tears formed on Pablo's lashes and Gordo Allende's savage face softened till his lips were smiling. And the old sheriff's faded eyes became dream-filled, gazing back, perhaps, to the day when he, too, had been tall and straight as a young pine of the forest, glorious in his youth and strength as was the tall singer of dreams and memories and the humble hopes of humble men.

The music ended in a crash of chords, and Slade stood smiling at the silence which preceded a roar of applause and shouts for another.

So he sang them another, a rollicking ballad of the hills and the plains and the rivers sparkling under the silver roses of the sky, and closed with a sweet and tender love song of old *Mejico* that caused more than one dance-floor girl to dab at her eyes with a wisp of lacy handkerchief.

"That young feller," said the marshal, "should be in Grand Opry, 'stead of followin' a cow's tail."

And in the darkness without, a dead man lay staring stonily at the sky.

Slade returned the guitar to its owner and rejoined Carmen at the table. She smiled at him tremulously, and when she spoke, her voice was low and throaty, " 'A thing of beauty is a joy forever.' True words indeed!"

"Thank you," Slade replied. "That's a real compliment."

"Just trying to even up for the many you pay me, only mine is sincere," she returned laughingly. "Now don't protest. It would take too long, and I wouldn't believe you, anyhow."

At that moment Pablo called her to the back room to check some papers. Slade sat smoking, and regarding the window which was no longer a black square, Pablo having closed the shutters. Suddenly a thought struck him. Gordo Allende was standing alone near the door. Slade got up and walked over to him.

"Gordo," he asked, "was that fellow following me before I entered the Lemming Inn?"

Gordo shook his head. "No," he replied. "He only appeared some little time after you entered. I had made myself comfortable on the porch of an *amigo* across the street and saw him slink around the corner to where he could watch the door of the Lemming Inn, even as I watched it. There were quite a few people on the street but he attracted my notice. As I said, he slinked and glanced furtively around, and loitered, smoking a cigarette. When *Cápitan* came out, he followed. As I said before, at a discreet distance."

Slade was silent a moment, then, "Gordo," he said, "unless I am mistaken there is an alley back of the Lemming Inn, similar to the one behind this *cantina.*"

"There is," Gordo answered. "I cannot be sure, but I think the *ladrone* came from that alley."

"I see," Slade said, his eyes thoughtful. "*Gracias,* and I'll be seeing you." He returned to the table to await Carmen.

She appeared shortly and seemed to have cast off her somber mood, for her eyes sparkled and the roguish smile touched her red lips.

"I've finished my work and said goodnight to Uncle Pablo," she announced. "It's late, dear, don't you think we should be going?"

"Guess we could do worse," he agreed.

Slade didn't pay much attention to his surroundings as they walked the shadowed streets for he knew that Gordo Allende and his young men, unseen, unheard, were never far off.

Carmen giggled as they turned into the flower-jeweled yard of the little house on Kansas Street.

"I hope they don't wait for you to come out!" she whispered.

13 . . .

The following day, Slade kept his promise to Shadow that he would get a chance to stretch his legs. Early afternoon found him riding swiftly eastward toward where the sun-washed crags of the Huecos frowned against the sky.

When he reached the point where the trail forked, five or six miles out of town, he turned into the little used track that trended north by east to pass close to the Hueco tanks. Frequently he gazed back the way he had come, but there were no indications that he was being followed.

He knew that where the trail drew near the tanks there were other and even less travelled tracks that led into the stony fastnesses of the mountains which were his goal.

"We may be going on just a wild goose chase, but I'm playing a hunch," he told Shadow. "A hunch that *amigo* Covelo has a secret hang-out somewhere among those rocks from which he stages his raids. Anyhow, we're going to play the hunch for a while. If nothing else, it's a nice day for a ride and you said you needed exercise. So don't go complaining."

Shadow snorted general disagreement to everything and paced on.

The sun was low in the sky by the time they covered the more than twenty miles from El Paso and neared the vicinity of the tanks. Here Slade rode warily, for this was outlaw land and had been, in one way or another, outlaw land since the dawn of history and before. From the rock-bound enclosures that formed natural fortresses, Apache bands, their hidden villages secure from enemies, raided into the rich middle valley of the Rio Grande and into Mexico beyond. Later, robbers and smugglers frequented the terrain, and still did. Winding about through the hills were furtive paths which had been beaten hard by myriads of moccasined feet over the course of the years, and by bare feet before the days of moccasins and Indians. Shallow caves and narrow overhung canyons offered protection from the elements and excellent hiding places for the brand of gentlemen who preferred to do most of their riding between the hours of sunset and dawn.

Early Spanish and Anglo-American explorers had availed themselves of the plentiful water supply in the numerous holes cut in the soft granite by wind and rain erosion, as did the immigrants of a later date and passengers of the Butterfield Stage Line which passed that way. Many pictographs adorned the sheltered rock walls, placed there by various tribes from prehistoric men up to the era of the occupation of the section by the Apaches, who were among the last to hole up there.

Slade turned Shadow to the left and rode on to the great clutter of giant rocks that lay scattered in wild confusion over a region nearly a mile long and a half a mile wide. Here he found pools of crystal-clear water. He also found tracks that led into the foothills. He studied them carefully, browsing about for some time. Finally he drew rein, hooked one long leg comfortably over the saddle horn and rolled a cigarette.

"Shadow," he said, after the brain tablet was going good, "horses have used some of these tracks recently, which means that somebody has been prowling around here. I've got a strong notion, now, that my hunch is a straight one." He glanced at the westering sun.

"But there's no sense in blundering around in the dark, so we'll jog on and try to get an early start tomorrow. A few miles along the main east-west trail are some small spreads. Maybe we can put on the nosebag at one of them and perhaps get some information of interest. I understand they have been losing cows of late. Looks like maybe *Señor* Covelo is dealing in a little wet beef along with his other activities. Well, we'll see."

He finished his smoke, carefully pinched out the butt and proceeded to make his way along the old track to where it joined the main trail, and turned east.

He rode steadily at a good pace and after a while began passing over rangeland, noticing clumps of good looking cows that bore a Swinging J brand. A few more miles and he sighted a small but well-built ranchhouse not far back from the trail. Drawing near, he spotted an old gent sitting on the porch, his boots propped on the railing. The owner of the boots let out a hospitable shout, "Light off, cowboy, and cool your saddle." Then, as Slade drew still nearer, the boots came to the floor with a thump and the oldster stood up.

"Hey!" he called. "Ain't you the young feller who's been lending Sheriff Hart such a good hand of late? Sure you are. Feller pointed you out to me in town. Come on in; soon be time to feed your tapeworm."

He let out a whoop and a wrangler came running from the barn. After being properly introduced to Shadow, he led the big black to a stall. Slade mounted the steps and accompanied the old gent into the house.

"My name's Jackson, Heth Jackson," his host introduced himself. "Believe your handle is Slade, ain't it? Right! Reckon you'll want to wash up before you eat. Water and soap and plenty of clean towels in back. Come along, Slade, I'll show you. The boys will be riding in any minute, now."

As they passed through the kitchen, the old cook, who was a Mexican, stared, then bowed low. Slade spoke a greeting in Spanish that caused the old fellow to beam.

Heth Jackson noted the bit of byplay but did not comment.

Slade enjoyed a good wash, combed his thick black hair and returned to the living room with Jackson who waved him to a comfortable chair and hauled out his pipe. Slade rolled a cigarette.

Jackson regarded him through the smoke. "How come you're riding this way, son?" he asked. "That is if you don't mind telling. Then, it's none of my business."

Slade told him, frankly, for there was no reason for concealment. Jackson puffed on his pipe and nodded.

"And you figure the hellion might be snoopin' about hereabouts?" he said, interrogatorily.

"I'm of the opinion that he has a hang-out somewhere other than El Paso, and the Huecos are the logical location," Slade replied. "His headquarters are in El Paso, all right, but if he runs true to outlaw form, he has a place where his bunch can lie low if it is advisable to do so, and from where they start their raids."

"Makes sense, all right," Jackson conceded.

"Understand cows have been widelooped in this section," Slade said.

"That's right," Jackson answered. "Couple of spreads over to the east of here have lost critters. So far, I've escaped, even though I am the closest to the river and to New Mexico, and I figure the hellions run 'em to the one or the other."

"Reasonable to think so," Slade agreed. "And nobody sighted the wideloopers?"

Jackson shook his head. "They're mighty slick operators," he replied. "Worked on stormy nights and sure know their business. Makes me think that you're right and it really is Covelo and his bunch, though it seems they sorta specialize in banks and stagecoaches."

"Plenty of money in rustling with the beef market what it is right now," Slade observed.

"You're darn right," Jackson agreed. "I'll admit I've been a mite worried of late. It's an easy run into the hills from my holding and it's a wonder they haven't made a try for my cows. I do try to keep 'em guarded, but you can't be everywhere at once, and the critters have a habit of clumping together around the water holes and the groves, especially in bad weather. They're sorta different from the old longhorns who went off mavericking by themselves or in twos and threes and weren't easy to round up. The improved stock is easy-going and no trouble to handle."

"But it can't be shoved along as fast as the longhorns," Slade pointed out.

"That's so," Jackson admitted.

Slade was silent for a moment, his eyes thoughtful, then, "That leads me to believe that they have a holding spot somewhere in the hills where they can corral the cows until they consider the time opportune to make a night run to the river or across the New Mexico Line."

"Sounds reasonable," Jackson conceded. He eyed his guest. "And I reckon you figure to look for that holding spot, right?"

"I do," Slade replied. "I hope to get an early start in the morning and do a little snooping around through the hills."

"Sorta risky, ain't it, riding around that way alone with such a bunch on the prowl?" Jackson disapproved.

"Not necessarily so," Slade replied lightly. "The chances are I won't meet anybody."

Jackson, still disapproving, shook his head but did not comment further.

"Think I hear the boys riding in," he said. "I'll mosey out and tell the cook to rattle his hocks. Take it easy and make yourself comfortable."

In the kitchen, Jackson asked of the cook, "You know that young feller, don't you, Esteban?"

"*Sí, patron,* I know him," the cook replied. "And it is the great honor to know *El Halcón.*"

"Hmm! *El Halcón.* Yep, that's what they called him," said Jackson. "Some funny stories about him going around, Esteban."

"Many are the stories that are told of *El Halcón,* some of them wondrous indeed," said Esteban.

"Who and what is he?" old Heth asked.

"He is *El Halcón,* the just, the compassionate, the friend of the lowly. A strange man, *patron,* perhaps more than a man; as to that I cannot say. Where there is evil or injustice *El Halcón* appears, from out of nowhere. When he departs, into the nowhere, evil and injustice have already departed, and peace and happiness have taken their place. His hand is ever outstretched to those in need of comfort or help, and his hand is strong."

Jackson nodded soberly. "Yes, I heard something like that about him, too," he admitted. "A hard man to go up against."

"In the hour of his wrath he is terrible, but he is good," said Esteban. Jackson nodded again.

"Understand he's sure been doing a fine job of thinning out the Juan Covelo bunch," he observed.

"Juan Covelo is doomed," Esteban stated with finality. "As soon should he give front to the Captain of God's Armies as to *El Halcón.*"

"Got a notion you're right," said Jackson. "Well, here come the boys. I'll lend you a hand with the stuff."

The hands rolled in shortly afterward. Slade liked their looks. The majority were gay, rollicking young fellows lusty with life and animal spirits, but there were a few oldtimers, including big Tim Barty, the range boss, who had been with Jackson for years.

Old Heth performed the introductions and they gazed with admiration, almost awe, at the already legendary figure whose exploits, some of them considered questionable in certain quarters, were the talk of the Southwest. Slade smiled at them, the flashing white smile of *El Halcón* that men, and women, found irresistible, and put them at their ease, and he was quickly accepted as one of the bunch.

Slade enjoyed an excellent dinner, after which there was a lengthy gabfest in the living room. Then everybody trooped off to bed, for it had been a long day and there was work to do on the morrow.

Jackson led his guest to a comfortable room on the second floor. "I'm an old batch," he announced. "Nobody in the house but me and Esteban. If you happen to want something, I sleep at the far end of the hall."

After a good night's rest and a hearty breakfast, Slade

was in the saddle early. Jackson gazed at the overcast sky and shook his head.

"Looks like we're in for a spell of falling weather," he commented.

"Yes, there appears to be a storm building up," Slade agreed, adding, "but I think it will hold off for a while."

"Hope to be seeing you soon again," Jackson said as Slade gathered up the reins.

He was due to see him again, sooner than he expected.

14 . . .

Leaving the Swinging J holding, Slade turned into the foothills of the Huecos. Hour after hour he rode, threading his way through brush-choked canyons, following dizzy ridges, working deeper and deeper into the mountains. Constantly he watched the movements of birds on the wing and little animals in the growth. And always he scanned the sky for that indubitable proof of human occupancy, smoke.

But the visibility was very bad, the sky lowering. Mist streamers swirled and eddied before a wind that blew stronger and stronger. He doubted if he would be able to identify smoke from the mist if he saw it. Altogether, it was a darn bad day for trying to locate a furtive quarry.

" 'Pears we're not getting much of a break," he remarked to Shadow, who was already thoroughly disgusted with thorns, loose stones that rolled under his irons, and things in general.

Shortly afterward they entered a narrow canyon walled by towering cliffs. And here Slade was abruptly heartened, his interest quickened. For the canyon floor showed evidence of the recent passage of horses and cattle.

"Horse, I believe we've hit it," he said. "Through this crack they run the cows. Perhaps we'll be able to back track the devils. That is, if the weather will just behave itself a little longer." The weather didn't.

It was late evening and the early night was not far off when the storm burst. The wind rose to gale force, lightning blazed, thunder crashed. The rain came down in sheets, driven like icy spears before the blast. Very quickly Slade lost all interest in running down outlaws. All he wanted was shelter for himself and his exasperated horse. He hugged the cliff to escape as much of the wind and rain as possible and sent Shadow on. In an incredibly short time, it was almost full dark. Slade swore, Shadow snorted equine profanity, the lightning flamed, the thunder roared, the wind bellowed.

Suddenly, directly ahead, Slade saw what appeared to be ghostly hands waving and beckoning to him through the tossing rain mists. What in blazes! He peered with narrowed eyes. The lightning flashed and he saw that the spectral beckoners were in reality hanging vines tossing in the wind. Behind their straggle was a black opening a dozen or so feet wide and nearly that in height.

He sent Shadow into it, the big black treading gingerly as stout chunks of withered vine and leaves and twigs blown in by the wind crunched under his hoofs. Almost instantly the bellow of the storm was muted and there was no wind and no rain. Slade struck a match, surveyed his surroundings and found that he was in a shallow cave that ran back into the cliff for half a dozen yards. He dismounted, scraped away the debris until he had a clear space of rock floor against one wall. Very quickly he got a fire kindled, feeding the blaze with chunks of vine until it was going well.

"This is perfect," he told Shadow. "Warm and dry, with plenty of fuel to keep the fire going. Let her rain! Let her blow! We're snug as a tick on a sheep's back."

He stripped off the rig and laid it and his slicker aside, spreading the saddle blanket near the fire to dry. His own blanket was in a waterproof roll behind the cantle. In the saddle pouches was a store of staple provisions—bacon, coffee, some eggs carefully wrapped to prevent breakage and a hunch of bread. Also a helping of oats for Shadow, a little flat bucket and a small skillet. Scraping another space clear, he dumped the oats; Shadow at once began munching and Slade set about preparing his own supper. There was plenty of water available, streaming down the vines, and soon coffee was bubbling in the bucket, bacon and eggs sizzling in the skillet.

He ate his simple meal with relish, then, after cleaning up the utensils, he stretched out on his blanket with a cigarette and reviewed the situation as it stood, for Shadow's benefit.

"Yes, I believe that they run the cows they wideloop from the spreads over to the east by way of this canyon to some place where they hold them in close herd before shoving them to the river or New Mexico. And if the blasted rain hasn't washed away all signs of their passing, we should be able to trail them to the holding spot. After that, we'll see."

His eyes were growing heavy, so he built up the fire, made himself comfortable beside it and went to sleep. Outside, the storm still bawled and bellowed, but the cave was warm and cosy; he was safe from the wind and the rain.

The dawn was breaking, a still dawn of blue and cloudless skies, when Slade suddenly awakened. For a moment he wondered what could have aroused him so suddenly. Then he realized it was a sound, a sound that steadily loudened and which he quickly identified as the rolling beat of many fast hoofs, accompanied by the querulous bleating of tired and disgusted cows.

The fire had burned to ashes and the cave was still dark, so he slipped to his feet and edged a little closer to the mouth.

Another moment and a string of cattle bulged into view. Slade estimated there were close to a hundred head. Tense, eager, he watched them stream past the cave.

After them, urging them to top speed, came half a dozen horsemen. Their faces were but whitish blurs in the dim light, but his pulses quickened as he saw that one was swathed in a hooded cloak that all but concealed his features. A cloak much like those the two pseudo brothers wore when they attempted to drygulch him in Juarez. Looked like maybe Covelo himself was one of the raiders.

After watching the band fade into the gloom—it was still shadowy in the narrow canyon—Slade slipped back into the depths of the cave. Working with smooth speed and efficiency, he got the rig on Shadow, rolled and strapped his blanket and mounted. He sent the black down the canyon at a moderate pace, straining his ears to catch any sound that would indicate that the wideloopers had slowed down. He did not dare get too near the band, for at close range odds of six to one would be a mite lopsided. The canyon was winding and there were places where he couldn't see fifty yards ahead.

Didn't matter, however. The only way he could hope to frustrate the raid was by allowing the bunch to get far ahead of him. He felt sure the canyon would lead to more open ground before long, for it ran through the straggling foothills that bulwarked the Huecos on the south. Peering and listening, he rode on, hoping at any moment to sight the canyon mouth and the open ground beyond.

The odds would still be six to one, but with Shadow to take him away from there if the going got too hot, his own unusual eyesight and his high-power Winchester, they would not be so lopsided as a numerical analysis appeared to indicate.

Now the sun was up, flooding the rain-washed sky with golden light. Slade peered ahead toward where the canyon curved sharply, and slowed Shadow a bit; he had no desire to meet the six coming back around the bend. He was fairly sure they had not spotted him standing near the mouth of the cave, but it wouldn't do to take chances.

He rounded the curve slowly. The canyon straightened out again, trending due west, and directly ahead he saw its mouth, with open, brush-dotted rangeland beyond. But just past the mouth the ground rose steeply, the crest of the rise, a few hundred yards farther on, glowing in the sunlight. And he did not speed up until he reached the crest and could see over it.

The open ground extended for more than two miles before the hills straggled down to flank the trail on either side. And a thousand yards or so to the front was the herd, the wide-loopers shoving it along. Slade's voice rang out, "Trail, Shadow! Trail!"

Instantly the great horse extended himself, his steely legs shooting back and forward like steam driven pistons. He tossed his head, slugged it above the bit and fairly poured his long body over the ground.

The thousand yards shrank to nine hundred, to eight. Now the outlaws were looking back over their shoulders. They had spotted him. One removed his hat and swung it in a circle.

"Waving us around, eh?" Slade muttered. "That makes it sure for certain; they don't want anyone approaching the herd, which wouldn't be the case were they just some punchers on a legitimate errand. Trail, fellow!"

Seven hundred yards! And now the outlaws were prodding the herd to greater speed. There was a flicker of flame, pale in the sunlight, a spurtle of smoke. A slug whined past, far to the left.

"Want to play rough, do you?" the Ranger said. "Just wait! Trail, Shadow!"

Another fifty yards! The outlaw rifles were blazing away. Some of the bullets came a mite too close for comfort. Slade estimated the distance. Once more his voice rang out, "Steady, Shadow!"

Instantly the black horse levelled off to a smooth, running-walk. Slade drew the Winchester from the saddle boot, clamped the butt to his shoulder. His eyes, cold as glacier ice, glanced along the sights.

The rifle bucked. Smoke and flame streamed from the

rock-steady muzzle. Almost instantly one of the wideloopers flung up his arms and fairly dived from the saddle. But when he hit the ground he stayed there.

Now slugs were whining past so close Slade felt the lethal breath of their passing. Again the steady muzzle. Again the flicker of flame and the spurtle of smoke. A second man lurched in his saddle but stayed erect. Slade shifted the Winchester muzzle the merest trifle, holding his fire a moment, endeavoring to single out the cloaked figure.

But the distance was great, the charging horsemen merged with the shapes of the laboring cattle; all forms looked alike. He brought the sights to bear and squeezed the trigger.

The rifle bucked. Another man toppled slowly,' swayed, seemed about to catch his balance, and fell, to lie motionless.

Then with that perception which is part of the mental outfit of the really keen and alert mind, the leader of the band saw that the game was up. Their grim pursuer could kill them all before they got him into the range of their average eyesight and less powerful weapons. Evidently at a word of command, the four remaining outlaws swerved and went racing around the herd. Slade speeded them on their way with lead but with little hope of scoring a hit. With Shadow still pacing smoothly along, he watched them pass the herd, swerve back into the trail and gallop on toward where the hills encroached on the trail. Alternating his gaze between the dwindling horsemen and the two motionless bodies on the ground, he slowed Shadow's pace.

The fleeing raiders kept going. Before Slade reached the forms in the trail, the riders vanished from his sight into the hills.

A single glance told *El Halcón* the two downed rustlers were both satisfactorily dead. Still watching the hills, he dismounted and gave them a quick once-over. Nothing outstanding about either, and their pockets divulged nothing of significance. Slade straightened up, studied the distant hills once more and turned his attention to matters close at hand.

The blowing cows, which he noted bore Heth Jackson's Swinging J brand, had jolted to a halt and were beginning to graze. The horses ridden by the dead outlaws had run a little ways then halted and were nosing the grass. They were excellent and docile animals and he had no trouble catching them.

Roping the bodies to the saddles and rounding up and turning the herd took time, especially since he had to keep a constant watch on the hills while he worked. The sun was well up the long eastern slant of the sky before the chore was finished and he got his charges under way, back toward where they came from.

He felt fairly well satisfied with the morning's adventure, but as he neared the canyon he was not quite so easy in his mind. If the outlaws were watching from the hills and charged in pursuit while he was in the gorge, the advantage might well be on their side. He shook his head as he sent the herd down the slope toward the shadowy opening between the cliffs. Abruptly he straightened in the saddle, the reloaded Winchester jutting to the front.

From the canyon mouth streamed nearly a dozen horsemen.

15 . . .

Rifle ready, Slade watched their approach. Then, with relief, he recognized in the foremost rider the tall form of Tim Barty, old Heth Jackson's range boss. He waved his hand for them to come on. A moment later they recognized him and speeded up, whooping, and volleying questions.

As they gathered around him, Slade told them what happened, to the accompaniment of profanity and admiring exclamations.

"Part of a shipping herd we planned to get together," said Barty, jerking his thumb toward the tired cattle.

"They weren't guarded?"

"Yes, Brett Nesbit was keeping an eye on 'em, but the hellions shot him from a thicket," Barty explained. "Guess they figured he was done for, but he wasn't; he was just creased. After they shoved off with the cows, he managed to fork his horse and hightail to the *casa*. We lit out after the sidewinders. Rain had stopped and it wasn't hard to trail them. Also, we figured they'd slide through that crack. But if it wasn't for you, feller, they'd have made the hills over to the west and there'd have been no following them there. You did the Old Man a mighty big favor; he needs the money for those cows to meet a note. He won't forget it, and we won't, either. Now what?"

"Now we might as well shove the cows back on pasture and then go on to the *casa*," Slade answered. "I think where I had the showdown with them is in El Paso County, so send a man to notify Sheriff Arch Hart. I'll remain at the ranchhouse till he shows up. Right now I could stand a sizeable surrounding; didn't have time for breakfast before I ambled after the devils."

"You'll get it, or anything else you may happen to hanker for," Barty declared with force. "Feller, you're a wonder! And you tackled the whole bunch of the horned toads, did for two of 'em and sent the rest skalleyhootin'! Yep, you're a wonder! And if you happen to want somebody killed, or the courthouse or a church burned down, just let me know. And that goes for the rest of the boys, too."

There was a general and noisy assent.

An astounded and happy man was Heth Jackson when the outfit rolled in with the news that the herd was back safe on pasture. He solemnly shook hands with Slade. And old Esteban the cook, said, "*Patron*, did I not tell you so?"

Whereupon he set about preparing a meal commensurate to the occasion. Slade, having had no breakfast, did full justice to it. But the hands, who also had had no breakfast, far outdid his finest efforts.

After a man was dispatched to El Paso to fetch the sheriff, Tim Barty engaged Slade in conversation.

"I figure it was Covelo, all right," said the range boss. "Brett said that as they pulled away with the herd, he yelped that blankety-blank-blank '*Buenas noches, Señor!*'"

"Covelo or one of his imitators," Slade replied. "Although his quick thinking and pulling out when he realized I had the range on them had the Covelo touch. On the other hand, the pair we packed to the house with us are pretty scrubby looking, not at all similar to others I'm pretty sure were members of his bunch who showed indications of intelligence above the average. However, it is likely that his original picked bunch has been pretty well thinned out and he has been forced to take whatever he could tie onto. Just conjecture, of course, but could be the answer.

"That is unless there's another of the same calibre as Covelo mavericking around in the section, which heaven forbid!"

"Amen!" Barty said fervently.

It was past sundown when Sheriff Hart arrived from El Paso.

"So, still thinnin' 'em out, eh?" he remarked to Slade. "How many of the hellions can there be, anyhow?"

"I think about all of his original bunch are out of the picture," Slade replied. "Come and take a look at that pair."

A lantern was procured and they repaired to the barn where the bodies were laid out. Hart examined them closely.

"Somewhat different from the others we tied onto, don't you think?" Slade observed.

"Uh-huh, they are," Hart agreed. "Brush poppin' scum I'd call them."

"I'm of the opinion that Covelo is just about scraping the bottom of the barrel," Slade said. "That is perhaps the reason he has turned to rustling all of a sudden; doesn't take much savvy to wideloop cows. But give him a little time and he'll get another able bunch together; an outlaw leader of his ability can always get followers."

"Got a notion his prestige has suffered something of a jolt of late, though," Hart commented.

"Yes," Slade agreed. "But his past exploits which displayed daring, shrewd planning and resourcefulness will not be forgotten. He has suffered some setbacks of late, but let him pull an outstanding chore and they *will* be forgotten; and that's just what I'm afraid he'll do if he isn't stopped. A few stolen herds properly disposed of mean ready money, which he may be in need of right now. And according to what Jackson told me, he's run off quite a few cows from the spreads over to the east. And money in the pocket is what counts with the owlhoot brand."

"You're right there," the sheriff agreed. "But just the same I figure you've got the hellion on the run. Incidentally, though, it means you've got to watch your step. He'll be after you, hot and heavy."

"Which may be just what I need," Slade replied. "Undue impulsiveness, like temper, clouds the judgment and may cause him to do something that will lay him wide open; I'm counting on that."

Sheriff Hart studied the Ranger for a moment. "Walt," he said, "have you any notion who Covelo really is? I got a feeling you have."

"Yes, I have," Slade admitted. "And not an iota of proof against the suspect to bolster my theory."

"Not ready to name any names yet, eh?"

"No, not yet. Very likely you'd just think I've all of a sudden gone loco. Yes, I have a definite theory as to who Covelo is, but so far it's just theory."

"Well, I've got one of my own," growled Hart. "I been doing a lot of thinking about that Mexican or half-Mexican who runs that rum hole, The Tank, and pretends to be Irish."

Slade laughed. "Joe Brian has a dark complexion, black eyes and black hair," he conceded. "But never to my knowledge have I seen a Mexican with sooty eyelashes, a long upper lip and a retroussé nose."

"Retro—retro—" sputtered the sheriff. "What sort of a nose is that?"

"Tip-tilted to you," Slade chuckled. "A nose that turns up. Joe Brian is Irish with a dash of black Scotch that gives him his hair, eyes and complexion. And I'll say right now, that you can definitely count Joe Brian out of the picture. He's a good saloonkeeper, and that's as far as he goes. He hasn't the brains to be Juan Covelo, or the disposition."

"I give up!" snorted Hart. "If you say it's so, I reckon it is. Guess I've been doing Brian an injustice by thinking that way of him."

"And that's why I prefer not to mention a name at present," Slade explained. "I might be doing somebody a grave injustice, for it is possible I am mistaken."

"I doubt it," said Hart. "You ain't in the habit of making those kind of mistakes. And when you decide to drop your loop, it'll be on the right critter."

"But it had better be a tight loop or the hellion will slide out of it," Slade answered. "Come on, Esteban is calling us to supper."

Early the following morning, Slade and the sheriff set out for El Paso, leading the outlaws' horses, with their bodies roped to the saddles. As they neared town, Slade turned in the saddle and gazed back at the frowning Huecos.

"I still think the sidewinder has a hole-up somewhere among those up-ended hunks of rock," he said. "Well, maybe I'll have better luck next time."

"I figure you had pretty good luck this time," Hart replied cheerfully. "And Heth Jackson sure figures he had good luck. Which I've a notion ain't the way Covelo is feeling right now."

"The devil always seems to get the breaks, though," Slade said. "I tried my darndest yesterday morning to line sights with him, but each time another of the bunch slid behind him or he blended with the cows."

"His luck, such as it is, won't hold," Hart predicted. "I'll bet my last peso on that."

"I think you're right, if luck is the right word for it, which I doubt," Slade said. "Clear thinking and recognizing opportunity is, I believe, the better explanation. Perhaps, though, being in a bad mood because of his recent setbacks, he may grow reckless and make a try for me that will give *me* opportunity; I hope so."

"I don't think you're ever really happy unless you're dodging lead," the sheriff sighed.

Being honest with himself, Slade had to admit that there was some justification for the remark. He did enjoy the fierce and hazardous game played with the outlaws, with death as the forfeit, especially when pitted against a man whose ruthless ingenuity and shrewdness made him an opponent to give even *El Halcón* pause. Well, to the winner the spoils of victory. To the loser, six feet of earth for a grave.

The bodies were laid out in the sheriff's office and, as before, citizens entered for a look at them. This time, however, there were some results. Several individuals were sure they had seen the pair hanging around the riverfront saloons. A bartender admitted serving them.

"Not that it means much," said Hart. "Their sort always drift down to those rum holes."

After the crowd had departed, Hart turned to Bob, the deputy.

"Everything quiet hereabouts?" he asked.

"Uh-huh, except for a row in that place with the loco name, the Lemming Inn," Bob replied. "Wasn't a very nice row."

"How's that?" asked the sheriff.

"A big planter was drunk and making a nuisance of himself," Bob explained. "Pawing the girls, shoving folks around. Hansen went over to him and in that nice quiet voice of his told him to behave himself. Feller hove a slap at him, slap didn't land. Then Hansen went to work on him. Didn't knock him out, like he could have done easy. Perceeded to cut his face to pieces with his fists. Face was just a bloody pulp. Finally he let him have one that put him on the floor, plumb out. Hansen walked over to him and kicked him in the face, twice. I figured it was time to interfere. I moved in and told Hansen to stop it. He turned on me, and his eyes were like a mad cat's. But I told him, 'Hansen, you're bucking the law now, and you ain't big enough to do that.'

" 'Guess you're right,' he said and told a couple of swampers to throw some water over the feller and shove him out. Which they did. He's a tough *hombre,* is Hansen, and mean as a striped snake when he gets his mad up."

"Would 'pear he is," Hart agreed soberly. "Sure don't look it, though, does he, Walt?"

"Appearances are often deceptive," was the Ranger's noncommittal reply.

"Sure are in his case," said Bob. "I figure he really enjoyed beatin' that poor devil's head off. Sorta gave me the creeps; was like a cat torturin' a mouse."

Slade nodded, his eyes thoughtful.

"I'm beginning to feel a mite lank," said the sheriff. "Suppose we amble over to the Lookout and surround a helpin' of chuck?"

Which they proceeded to do.

"And now what?" Hart asked as he pushed back his empty plate and took a sip of coffee.

"After I finish my coffee and have a cigarette, I think I'll go down to Pablo Montez's *cantina*," Slade replied.

"A good notion," nodded the sheriff. "I wouldn't be surprised if the little gal is a mite worried."

Carmen was worried, plenty worried. "You'd drive any woman crazy," she scolded.

"Coming from you, that remark is not exactly original," Slade answered, his eyes laughing.

"Perhaps not," she conceded. "But this time I mean it in a different way. You're the limit! You vanish without saying a word to anybody. What happened?"

Slade told her. She drew a deep and shuddering breath.

"I believe you just go looking for trouble," she declared.

They were alone at an isolated table. From a cunningly concealed secret pocket in his broad leather belt, Slade drew the famous silver star set on a silver circle, the feared and honored badge of the Texas Rangers, and cupped it in his hand.

"Not the first time you've seen it," he reminded her. "You know what it means."

"Yes, I know what it means," she said slowly. "What a life you live! And I really think you enjoy it."

"I do," he admitted. "Which is why no woman should take me too seriously."

Her eyes danced. "Perhaps not," she conceded, "but, hard as it is on the nerves, I'll take a chance."

They laughed together.

Pablo joined them and Slade repeated the story of the thwarting of the widelooping for his benefit.

"Good work," he said. "I know old Heth Jackson well; he's a real oldtimer hereabouts, like myself, and he's all right. In the morning I'll go have a look at those bodies; might be able to tie them up with something. I'll take Gordo Allende with me."

"A good idea," Slade agreed. "Do that."

"I still have work to do," Carmen said. "Are you going to stay here? Will take me an hour or so."

"I think I'll stroll around a bit," Slade replied. "I'll be back a little later."

"And please stay out of trouble for a change," she sighed.

"I'll try," he promised.

16 . . .

After gradually working his way to Santa Fe Street, Slade entered the Lemming Inn and occupied a table. The waiter who had served him on the occasion of his former visits hurried to take his order. Glancing about, Slade failed to spot the owner.

"Hansen around?" he asked casually. The waiter shook his head.

"Ain't come in yet. Been away quite a bit of late. Wasn't here night before last, all night. Came in late yesterday; said he'd been out riding. Clothes looked like it, dust all over, and he's usually neat as a pin. Had a row with a trouble maker who was bothering everybody. Finished him off proper. Maybe you heard about it?"

"I heard there was a ruckus here last night," Slade replied evasively.

"The boss is all right, but don't get him started," said the waiter. "He's bad if you do. Reckon he has to be to run a place like this. Usually everything goes along smooth, but now and then some jigger with a snort too many under his belt ruffles things up. The boss can take care of 'em though. Most of the time all he has to do is talk to him and edge 'em out, but not always. Reckon you know the sort I'm talking about—find 'em everyplace."

"Yes," Slade admitted. "And, as you say, they are to be found everywhere."

The waiter nodded. "Yes, the boss is hard when he needs to be," he repeated. "Expect he gets it from his dad. I heard *he* was a bucko mate on a big Scandinavian windjammer, as they call the sailing ships. Guess you have to be hard to hold down a job like that."

"You do," Slade agreed. "Young Hansen didn't take to the sea?"

"Understand he was on it for a while," answered the waiter. "Got tired of it, I reckon, and opened up a place in California, or so I heard. Didn't like it there and came over this way. I think he brought a few of his shipmates along with him; guess they drifted elsewhere. Back to sea, the chances are. I never met any of 'em, and maybe it was just talk and they weren't really sailors. Although I guess sailors do come back to land sometimes."

"Quite frequently, especially after they begin to get along in years," Slade said, leaving an opening for the loquacious waiter to continue, for he found his gabble quite interesting.

At that moment, however, the man under discussion entered and the conversation abruptly ceased.

Hansen glanced around, nodded shortly to Slade, and walked quickly to the far end of the bar, where he began speaking to the head bartender. The waiter joined them. Hansen said something to him and he hurried to the kitchen.

Studying the owner, Slade thought that Hansen looked distraught and nervous. His gaze continually roved about the room, as if he were seeking somebody.

The waiter reappeared with a couple of sandwiches and a cup of coffee. Hansen ate standing, still engaging the head bartender in conversation. From time to time he glanced at the swinging doors.

A moment later, a man entered who also glanced about as if in search of someone. His gaze rested on *El Halcón's* face, his eyes narrowed slightly and he seemed to hesitate. Abruptly, however, he appeared to change his mind and strode to where Hansen stood. He was a tall man, heavily built, and he walked with a peculiar rolling gait that caused Slade to instantly deduce that he was or had been a sailor. He spoke to Hansen in a low voice. The saloonkeeper nodded and motioned to the waiter who brought more sandwiches and more coffee of which the newcomer partook. The bartender placed a filled glass at his elbow. Wiping his lips, he tossed off the drink at a gulp, turned to Hansen and said a word or two. The pair left the saloon together. Hansen nodded to Slade again but did not pause. *El Halcón* watched them go and then ordered coffee.

For a few minutes Slade remained at the table, heavy with thought. Chiefly he was wondering where the devil Hansen and his seafaring companion were headed for, and how to find out.

To attempt to trail the pair from the Lemming Inn was ridiculous; he was sure to be spotted. Suddenly he had an inspiration; he turned to the waiter who was hovering about and tried a long shot.

"Any idea where there's a good stable hereabouts?" he asked. "I'd like to move my horse down this way."

"Why, there's a good one right over on the alley back of Chihuahua Street," the waiter replied. "The boss keeps his horse there, and so does the head bartender. Reckon you could get a stall for your cayuse there."

"Thank you," Slade replied. "I'll look it up. Another cup of coffee, please."

The waiter nodded, and when he returned with the coffee he handed out what Slade considered a valuable bit of information.

"Guess the boss is off again," he remarked. "He told Lafe, the head bartender, that he was going to drop in at a place up on South Stanton Street and then he aimed to take a ride to visit some friends. Didn't figure to get back tonight. He's a busy man."

"Appears to be," Slade agreed. He took his time about drinking the coffee; if what he had in mind would work, there was no need to hurry. Finally, tipping the waiter generously and saying so long, he departed. He did not turn toward Chihuahua Street but walked steadily until he reached Pablo's *cantina*. There, as he expected, he found Gordo Allende and several of his young men. Tersely he told Gordo what he had in mind.

"Keep an eye on the stable," he concluded. "When Hansen leaves there, if he does, and I think he will, try and learn which way he's headed. No, don't try to follow him, just find out, if possible, which way he turns when he leaves town. He might be headed for Juarez, but I don't think so. I figure he'll take either the east trail to the Huecos or the southeast trail toward Van Horn. In a way, I'm playing a hunch, but I believe it's a straight one."

"Assuredly, *Cápitan*," Gordon replied. "He will not leave El Paso without us knowing which way he goes. You can depend on us, *Cápitan*."

Slade felt certain he could. The young men would be stationed at strategic points and would note every move made by Hansen and his companion, and Hansen would not notice *them*. They could be as inconspicuous as shadows on a cloudy day when they took the notion to.

"I'll be at the sheriff's office," he told Gordo.

Satisfied with the way things were working out, so far, he entered the back room where he found Carmen just finishing up her work. She gave him a searching look.

"You're up to something—I can see it in your eyes," she declared.

"Nothing serious," he returned lightly. "I'm going to the sheriff's office now for a while, but I'll be seeing you."

Her eyes were somber as she watched him leave.

Slade did not go straight to the office. Instead, he repaired to the stable where Shadow was quartered and got the rig on the big black.

"I'll be coming for him soon," he told the keeper. "I flipped the bit out so you can let him have a helping of oats and give him water with a little whiskey in it."

At the office, he quickly acquainted the sheriff with what he had in mind. Hart stared at him.

"Hansen!" he exclaimed. "So that's the hellion you've had in mind all the time, eh?"

"Yes," Slade replied. "Now I'm so convinced that Gus Hansen is Juan Covelo that I feel free to mention it to you. Yes, he's Covelo, all right. The son of a Scandinavian ship's officer who perhaps did marry the daughter of a Yaqui chief, as the story goes. Hansen inherited his appearance from his father, who doubtless was a blonde Norse. It will work out that way some times. Bob clinched the case against him, so far as I was concerned, when he told us of the savage beating he gave that poor devil of a drunken planter. It was an example of the streak of senseless, sadistic cruelty for which Covelo is notorious. He wears a hooded cloak to hide his yellow hair. His eyes are such a dark blue as to seem black to the casual observer. There are other points I'll tell you about later."

Hart swore and tugged his mustache. "Guess you're right," he said. "Come to think of it, the hellion does have a sorta funny look about him. I noticed his eyes once myself when an argument in his place kinda upset him; they were bad. And if Gordo learns which way he goes, you figure to trail him?"

"That's what I plan to do," Slade replied. "I hope to catch him red-handed at something, for no matter what I believe, I still have nothing against him that would stand up in court; a smart lawyer would make a laughing stock of me if I tried it."

"How about Bob and me going with you?" Hart suggested. Slade shook his head.

"I figure I can handle this chore better alone," he answered. "One is less liable to be spotted than two or three."

"You may find some bad odds against you."

"Yes, but I figure I'll have the advantage of surprise and position on my side, just as was the case in the widelooping attempt."

Hart sighed and shook his head. "You usually seem to know what you're talking about, but I still say you'll be taking one devil of a chance," he protested. "Sounds plumb loco to me."

"Often what appears to be taking a chance is the safest course," Slade pointed out. "The element of surprise is always highly important, and I'm of the opinion that the last thing Hansen will think of is that I'll be trailing him."

The sheriff still did not look convinced, but he raised no further objection.

Dusk was falling when Gordo Allende entered the office.

"Southeast trail, he and three others," he stated laconically. "Me, I too play the hunch and watch that trail myself."

"How long ago?" Slade asked.

"The fifteen, maybe the twenty minutes," Gordo replied. Slade rose to his feet.

"Thank you, Gordo," he said. "You've been a big help."

"It is the pleasure and the honor to lend the helping hand to *El Halcón*," Gordo said. "Good hunting, *Cápitan*."

17 . . .

Leaving the still dubious sheriff, Slade hurried to the stable and led Shadow forth. He swung into the saddle and by way of Texas Street soon reached the southeast trail which led to Van Horn and on east to Pecos, with a fork trending south from Van Horn to Marfa.

Not that he believed Hansen and his followers would have such a lengthy journey in mind. He was of the opinion that they contemplated a raid on one of the ranches south of the valley farms and grape arbors. And he was confident that he could overtake the bunch and spot them without being spotted himself. Later there would be a moon, and the sky was clear. Lounging easily in the saddle, he sent Shadow forward at a fast pace, constantly scanning the trail ahead, although he did not believe Hansen and his devils would draw rein until they were past the farmhouses and onto the rangeland beyond. It was logical to think they would continue without pause through the cultivated area, not wishing to attract attention to themselves. However, it would not do to take chances.

The moon rose, before whose chaste glory the stars paled their ineffectual fires and all the world was wreathed in ghostly light under which objects were distorted and unreal, clumps of thicket standing out as solid blocks of blackness, hollows brimming with elusive shadows, the trail ahead a wanly glowing ribbon.

The scene was beautiful but drear, possibly from excess of beauty. It called to Slade's mind that most weird of the lyric legends of Ireland, "The Curse of Mora."

"The fretted fires of Mora blew o'er him
    in the night;
He thrills no more to loving, nor weeps
    for past delight.
For when those flames have bitten, both
    joy and grief take flight—

And through the sleeping silence his feet
must track the tune,
When the world is barred and speckled with
silver of the moon!"

Yes, on such a night as this anything could happen. Before the dawn, *his* feet might well tread the path to that lovely bourne from which no traveller returns.

Oh, well! All in the day's work. He shrugged his broad shoulders and rode on, watchful and alert.

Finally he passed the last farmhouse. The rangeland stretched before him, eerie, mysterious in the unnatural light pouring down from the star-spangled sky. On his right was the railroad line, no great distance off. Once a long freight rumbled past, then a local passenger train, both speeding to clear the track for the Sunrise Limited that already was booming along from Sierra Blanca.

He began passing clumps of grazing cattle and, a little later, his keen eyes spotted his quarry far, far to the front, riding at a good pace but apparently in no hurry. Where were they headed for? Very likely, he thought, for some spread a little farther on, where possibly a shipping herd was being assembled, not unusual at this time of the year. Or so he surmised, for, after all, he admitted he was just following a hunch, although he believed it to be a straight one.

Generally speaking, it was. But in detail it was wide of the mark indeed.

He felt fairly sure that so long as he kept his present distance the four riders could not see him in the deceptive moonlight. In fact, he believed he could risk getting a little closer.

Now the four were riding across a level space that ended in a long and gentle rise with a rounded crest. Slade drifted along after them, watched them breast the rise, reach the crest and vanish from his sight over it. He speeded up a bit. Finally he neared the crest, slowing Shadow as a precautionary measure against the possibility that the quarry had also slowed down, or paused for some reason or other. He topped the rise and abruptly reined in. Before him was a descending slope that levelled off to a wide and open moon drenched expanse. Far ahead was a belt of thicket, not very wide, that extended northward for several miles and into which the trail flowed. And the quarry was nowhere in sight.

Slade estimated the breadth of the thicket, beyond which was open ground again, and was certain that the horsemen he was trailing had had ample time to pass through it. If they had negotiated the belt of growth, they would undoubtedly still be within his range of vision. But where the devil were they? The obvious answer was that they had paused within the growth.

But why? Here there were no cattle, no apparent reason for them to draw rein. He studied his surroundings with care. To the right, the twin steel ribbons of the railroad still gleamed in the moonlight, with the river beyond, the railroad skirting the south edge of the growth.

Endeavoring to analyze the situation, Slade found himself in something of a quandary. Did the bunch head north through the thicket? He shook his head. To try to negotiate that thorny tangle for any great distance would be an act of lunacy. Then came the decidedly disquieting thought— had they spotted him and were they holed up waiting? If so and he attempted to cross the open space bathed in moonlight, he'd be settin' quail for fair.

So what the devil to do? And why the devil were Hansen and his followers remaining concealed in the thicket? He was convinced in his own mind that they had not spotted him, but, he was forced to admit, there remained an element of doubt, and did he make a mistake it would very likely be the last one he made on this earth. In fact, the only sensible thing to do was stay right where he was until he learned something definite.

His gaze roved over the thicket, constantly returning to the trail that flowed on east and south beyond the belt of brush. He studied the westerly edge of the growth. Perhaps the hellions would turn southwest to the river, but why? Did they intend to cross into Mexico? Not impossible, but again, why?

Abruptly his gaze centered on the southwesterly fringe where the belt of growth ended just before reaching the railroad right-of-way. He was positive he had seen movement there, a merging and separating of shadows, grotesque, unreal in the moonlight. Very faint, but nevertheless movement.

The movement ceased. The slow minutes dragged past. Now the Ranger was thoroughly puzzled. There seemed to be no sense to the bizarre performance. But Juan Covelo did not do things that didn't make sense, and Slade was convinced that down there in the brush was Juan Covelo with a hooded cloak concealing his yellow hair and his eyes glinting darkly in the shadow of his hatbrim.

Thin with distance sounded the wail of a locomotive's whistle. Again, this time louder. Far to the southeast a flicker of light appeared, the engine's headlight beam, steadily becoming more apparent. And abruptly *El Halcón* understood.

"Shadow!" he exclaimed. "The hellions are going to make a try for the Limited! Trail, feller, trail!"

Instantly the great black shot forward, his hoofs drumming the surface of the trail. Slade estimated the distance to where the outlaws were waiting at the edge of the brush close to the steel ribbons of the railroad. His gaze flickered to that onrushing headlight beam. Now he could see the shimmer of lights that were the coach windows. They were close, devilish close, and drawing closer by the second, and he was still far off.

He wondered fleetingly if the outlaws could see the trail from where they crouched at the edge of the brush. If they could, he'd doubtless hear about it any instant. However, he counted heavily on their attention being centered on the oncoming train, the rumble of which now reached his own ears. He could also hear the staccato booming of the exhaust. The Limited was late and making up time. But unless he could reach the thicket in time she would be a darn sight later. He glanced again at the advancing beam of light. No hope of preventing the wreck that appeared inevitable. All he could hope to do was thwart the intended robbery of the express car. That was what the devils had in mind, all right. Very often, he knew, the express car packed a large sum of money consigned to an El Paso bank or some other bank farther west. Hansen had somehow learned what the train was carrying today and was out to tie onto it. Not too hard for a supposedly respectable businessman to obtain such information. Yes, that was it: robbery, with murder incidental. Maybe he would be in time to prevent the murders. He fervently hoped so as the thicket loomed large and dark and the trail flowed back under Shadow's drumming hoofs. He urged the black to greater speed, swerving him from the trail toward the railroad.

Shadow responded gallantly, giving his all. Now the belt of brush was close. But closer still was that blazing headlight beam. Whatever was going to happen would happen in a matter of seconds.

It did! A blinding yellow glare paled the moonlight. Slade's ears rang to the thundering roar that accompanied it. The booming exhaust snapped off, followed by a screaming of brake shoes against the wheels.

But they could not stay the speeding train. The locomotive crashed into the hole blown under the tracks by the exploding dynamite and flipped over on its side with a bellow of steam from broken pipes. The express car teetered crazily, plunged downward, but stayed erect.

From the brush darted four men. Something trailed sparks through the air and exploded against the express car door, shattering it. The outlaws raced toward the smashed door. Slade's voice rang out, "Steady, Shadow, steady!"

The great black levelled off to his smooth running walk. Slade streaked his Winchester from the saddle boot and opened fire.

One of the owlhoots plunged forward on his face. His companions whirled to face the Ranger. Flame flickered. Lead whined past, close. Slade took deliberate aim, pulled the trigger again.

A second man went down. The two remaining spun about and sped for the shelter of the thicket. A moment later they reappeared, mounted, racing their horses along the edge of the growth to the open trail beyond.

"So! figure on getting into the clear, eh?" *El Halcón* growled. "You won't do it, not if I know old Shadow. Trail, feller!"

At that instant it happened. Shadow plunged a reaching front foot into a badger hole. He reared back desperately to save his leg.

He did save it, but couldn't save himself from falling. Slade kicked his feet free from the stirrups as his mount went down. He was hurled from the saddle to strike the ground with great force.

For moments he lay half stunned, lights flashing before his eyes, his limbs refusing to function. By the time he managed to struggle erect, the two wreckers were out of sight.

"And I'll bet my last peso one of them is Covelo!" he exclaimed in utter exasperation and disgust.

18 . . .

Slade's first thought was for his horse. Shadow had also regained his feet and was snorting and holding up one front hoof. Slade hurried to him. To his great relief, a quick examination of the injury showed the leg was not broken, only bruised and strained.

"Think you can make it, feller?" Slade asked anxiously. Shadow's snort signified that he could. He proved it by putting his foot down and pacing alongside his master. He limped a little, but otherwise appeared to be okay.

Shouts were sounding from the wreck, which was less than a hundred yards distant. Loud, too, were the yells and screams of injured or frightened passengers. A lantern carried by a blue-clad trainman bobbed in Slade's direction. He walked forward to meet the advancing conductor, who let out a whoop as soon as he was within hailing distance.

"Blazes! Cowboy, where did you come from? Anyhow, you sure showed up at the right time. Another minute and the blankety-blank blanks would have been in the express car."

"Anybody badly hurt?" Slade called back.

"Can't tell yet for sure," replied the conductor. "Engineer and fireman climbed out of that mess cussin', so I reckon they made it. Bleedin' a bit, but didn't seem too bad. Don't know about the express messenger. Sure hope he wasn't close to the door when that stick of dynamite cut loose."

"How about the passengers?" Slade asked.

"Don't know yet," the conductor repeated. "Some cuts and bruises and maybe a busted bone or two, I reckon. Luckily the coaches stayed on the iron. The hogger had slowed her quite a bit for the curve, or I reckon the whole blankety-blank shootin' match would have turned over. I saw you fall and thought you were done for. You didn't get hit?"

"Horse stepped in a badger hole," Slade explained briefly.

"We got shook up a bit, that's all. Let's learn if there are any serious injuries."

"I'll bet a hatful of pesos there would have been if it wasn't for you," the conductor declared grimly. "That was a bunch of killers or I miss my guess." Slade nodded sober agreement.

The engineer and fireman had suffered minor cuts and bruises, and the fireman's arm had been slightly scalded by escaping steam.

"I'll take care of you shortly," Slade said. "I want to have a look at the express messenger."

His fears for that worthy were quickly relieved. Swinging into the car by way of the shattered door, he found the messenger smoking a cigarette and swearing.

"Knocked me pizzle-endwise when the dynamite let go, but I wasn't close to the door," he replied to Slade's question. "If I had been, reckon I wouldn't be here to tell you about it."

Slade glanced at the big iron safe bolted to the floor against one wall.

"Much in that box?" he asked in low tones.

The messenger hesitated, shot him a keen glance. "Ain't supposed to mention it, but I reckon you got a right to know," he answered. "Close to a hundred thousand pesos; would have been a darn nice haul. The Company will have something to say to *you* about saving it."

"Consigned to El Paso?"

"That's right," said the messenger.

"Thank you," Slade said, and swung to the ground, leaving the messenger staring after him.

A brakeman came hurrying from the coaches. "Nobody bad hurt," he told the conductor. "Mighty lucky Ad was slowing her before she hit that hole. Folks back there are looking after each other; some oldtimers aboard who know what to do." He gazed admiringly at Slade.

"You sure did a good chore, feller," he added, "a raunchin' good chore."

"I suppose you have a telegraph instrument aboard?" Slade said to the conductor. "We'll cut in on the wire if you have."

"Yep, we got one back there," replied the conductor. "Get it, Bill." The brakeman nodded and hurried back along the line of coaches.

"You can send?" Slade asked the conductor. "If you can't, I can."

The conductor stared a little. "Sorta unusual for a cowboy

to know how to handle a key," he commented. "Yep, I can tap out enough to tell 'em to get the heck here in a hurry."

"Summon the wreck train from Alpine, and tell El Paso to rush some coaches down here to take care of the passengers," Slade directed. "And have them notify the sheriff."

"Okay," said the conductor, "but it's going to be a chore, cuttin' in on the wire," he added, gazing dubiously at the tall telegraph pole at the edge of the right-of-way.

"I'll take care of that chore," Slade told him.

"Reckon there ain't anything much you can't do," chuckled the conductor. Slade smiled and did not comment.

His next step was to examine the bodies of the slain wreckers, hoping against hope that one would prove to be Gus Hansen, or at least the seafaring man he had seen in his company.

He was doomed to disappointment. The dead men proved to be ordinary appearing individuals he had never seen before.

"Ornery lookin' scuts," growled the conductor, glaring at the still forms.

"About as to be expected," Slade replied and turned his attention to the engineer and fireman, who were sitting on a crosstie and expressing their opinion of things in general in terms that smoked. He quickly decided that their injuries were of little account. Some soothing salve smeared on the cuts and the fireman's scalded arm took care of them for the time being.

By the time he had finished the treatment, the brakeman returned with the telegraph instrument. Slade went up the pole hand over hand, trailing the wires after him. He quickly cut in on the line and the conductor managed to make Alpine and El Paso understand what was needed. Slade unhooked the instrument wires and descended. The conductor observed the wreck.

"Ain't the first time one like this happened," he observed. "A year or so back some hellions wrecked and tried to rob the Midnight Flyer with dynamite. Come to think of it, a cowboy feller busted up that one, or so I was told."

Slade smiled. He did not deem it necessary to mention that he was the "cowboy feller" in question.

"The horses that pair rode should be somewhere nearby," he remarked. "Bring your lantern and let's see if we can locate them."

They did without much difficulty, good looking critters

standing patiently in the edge of the brush a little ways to the east. Slade removed the rigs and left them to fend for themselves. They immediately began to graze.

"And they can get water from the river," he told the conductor. "Now I wonder if your dining car is still operating? I could use a cup of coffee about now, if one is available."

"There'll be one available, and as many more as you want, if I have to bust a head," the conductor declared grimly. "Come along."

"Just as soon as I flip the bit out of my horse's mouth and loosen the cinches so he can tie onto a surrounding of grass in comfort," Slade said, and proceeded to suit the action to the word.

The dining car chef proved to be an elderly colored man who appeared little affected by the night's hectic happenings.

"Done had my kitchen messed up too many times in my day to pay much mind to such bobberties," he explained to Slade. "I just clean up and let the brains do the worryin'. Here's your coffee, suh, and I got some prime roast beef for you, too. Nope, I don't want no pay. It's a plumb pleasure to serve a real gentleman."

"Thank you," Slade replied, his cold eyes abruptly all kindness.

The coaches from El Paso arrived shortly after Slade finished his meal. With them came Sheriff Hart and Bob, the chief deputy. Hart gave him a searching glance.

"You all right?" he asked.

"Fine as frog hair," Slade replied. He drew the sheriff and deputy aside and told them just what happened.

"And the hellion got away," growled Hart.

"Yes," Slade said. "I'm almost ready to believe he has a charmed life. Everything seems to break in his favor."

"He'll end up with his blasted neck breaking, of that I'm sure for certain," Hart predicted. "I knew darn well when word of the wreck came in that you'd be mixed up in the business somehow. Didn't know what might be in the wind, so I made 'em hook a stall car ahead of the caboose and brought our horses along in case we might need 'em."

"Good!" Slade said. "Now we can give Shadow a lift to town. Leg doesn't seem to bother him much, but he'll be better for not using it anymore tonight."

"That's right," agreed the sheriff. "Bring him along and load him into the car; they'll soon be ready to roll. We'll hit El Paso earlier than we would on horseback. Reckon the wreck train will be a while yet getting up from 'Alpine. Well, you did a pretty good night's work."

"Yes, but I blundered badly," Slade said as they walked Shadow to the car. "Guess I had cattle on the brain to the exclusion of all else. I was convinced that they intended to raid one of the spreads and governed myself accordingly. Didn't catch on to what they really had in mind until the last minute. Otherwise I might have been able to prevent the wreck."

"Uh-huh, and maybe got yourself killed trying to," grunted Hart. "I figure things worked out mighty well. A busted up engine ain't so much. A heck of a lot better than somebody taking the big jump, which very likely would have happened if you hadn't busted up their plans. Covelo would have been mighty apt to murder the express messenger, if he ran true to form, and I've a notion he was in a killing mood. Sure is now, I'll bet, so watch your step. I got a feeling he's the sort to commit suicide if he can just take the other feller along with him. Like John Ringo over in Tombstone you were telling me about."

"Could be," Slade conceded. "A warped brain does strange things. Not much doubt but that Ringo did finally commit suicide, after trying his best to kill some others first. But Ringo was splendidly brave and, despite his faults, a man of high principles. He couldn't shoot in the back, take undue advantage of anybody or do anything wantonly cruel."

"Which sure don't go for that cat-eyed hellion you're up against," Hart growled. "He likes to see people suffer, and he wouldn't know a high principle if he met it in the middle of the road. He's just what a hyderphobia skunk is supposed to be and generally ain't. Well, here's the stall car; walk on air, cayuse."

With Shadow cared for and comfortably stalled, Slade and the sheriff found seats in one of the coaches.

"I'll arrange to have those other two critters picked up," Hart said, apropos of the dead outlaws' horses. "Here we go; won't be overly late getting into town. Reckon you'll be heading for Pablo's *cantina*, eh?"

"Yes, I suppose so," Slade admitted. "Chances are they'll be a mite worried about me there."

"Yep, expect *she* will be," Hart commented dryly. Slade smiled and changed the subject.

"You asked me how I got a line on Hansen, in the first place," he resumed. "Just a few little incidents, apparently trivial, but in the aggregate highly significant. As I have often mentioned, there is no such thing as a criminal physiognomy—you can't judge by facial appearances. But there always seem to be certain characteristics peculiar to that element which fall into a pattern. One is an apparently irresistible urge to obtrude themselves into a situation. When I first visited the Lemming Inn, I knew very well he was studying me and endeavoring to conceal the fact. I didn't think much of it at the time—my *El Halcón* reputation had gotten around and it was logical for an owner to look somewhat askance at a person with such a reputation. However, he pretended not to know me. And that is where he made a slip."

"How's that?" asked the sheriff.

"The night those two hellions disguised as brothers tried to drygulch me, Hansen put in an appearance at Miguel's *cantina* in Juarez right afterward. There, with an air of innocence, he asked Miguel my name, which I am positive he already knew. Get the point?"

"Guess I do," nodded Hart. "Sort of in the nature of a cover-up, eh?"

"Exactly," Slade replied. "That suddenly aroused my interest in him. Why did he do it? Why did he have to cover up? When a man lies, especially needlessly so, or so it would appear, he will usually bear watching. Then later that night one of the Covelo bunch was murdered on the bridge approach, and *'Buenas noches, Señor!'* was called right after the shooting. I was already convinced that Covelo had lived in California and heard the story of Joaquin Murrieta, the notorious California outlaw. That caused me to do a little thinking also, after I concluded that the man was one of the Covelo bunch. But what caused me to really think seriously about Hansen were his fingernails."

"Fingernails?" the sheriff repeated in bewildered tones.

"That's right," Slade said. "I got a good look at them when he approached my table in the Lemming Inn. You will recall you told me that it was generally believed that Covelo was the son of a seafaring man, a ship's officer, doubtless of Scandinavian blood, by a Yaqui mother. To which I didn't give much thought at the time. Hansen I had already decided was of Norse ancestry, presumably a blonde Norse— he sure looks the part. But when I got a look at his nails, they showed something else that all of a sudden was significant."

"What?"

"They were the nails of an Indian. There is a decided

difference between the nails of a white person and a colored person; it is quite apparent. The difference between the nails of a white and a red is not so pronounced, but it can be detected by close scrutiny."

"Uh-huh, by such eyes as yours," grunted the sheriff.

Slade smiled and continued, "There was, I felt, a rather remarkable, too remarkable, instance of coincidence. Would seem that both Covelo and Hansen had a Norse father—which I later learned to be so where Hansen was concerned—and an Indian mother. That set me thinking very seriously about Gus Hansen."

"Anything else?" asked the sheriff.

"Yes, something I considered also significant," Slade replied. "Whenever anything was pulled, Hansen was away from his place of business; that I learned from a talkative waiter in the Lemming Inn, who told quite a few more things. Also, Juan Covelo was singularly able to learn where there was a chance for a good haul—take the try on the Limited tonight; she rarely packs anything like a hundred thousand dollars. Which, I felt, meant that as somebody else he had good contacts here in town, the kind of contacts a successful businessman with a good reputation would have. I'll repeat what I said before, Hansen continually forced himself into the picture in one way or another."

"I can see it, now that you pointed it out," said Hart.

"Of course I was interested in all newcomers, especially those who had recently set up in business of one sort or another," Slade resumed. "That's why I visited the Lemming Inn and The Tank, just as I visited other places which I quickly discarded as of no consequence. The Tank and the Lemming Inn I considered worthy of consideration. You were a mite suspicious of Joe Brian, but I quickly dismissed him as a suspect. He just didn't appear to be the proper type; he was too open and frank. He knew I was *El Halcón*, didn't make any bones about saying so, wondered what I was doing here and discussed it out loud. Hansen was just the opposite.

"And there were a few other small matters to bolster my belief. That box of Copenhagen snuff we found in the pocket of one of the Covelo bunch—highly unusual for the rangeland, but favored by seamen, especially those of Norse extraction. Hansen evidently brought some of his bunch with him from California, where doubtless he operated till things got too hot. It set me to wondering. And the hooded cloak he wears, to conceal his yellow hair, without a doubt, and to help make his dark blue eyes look black, thus to further the Juan Covelo fable which he started. A simple disguise, and effective because of its simplicity; better than a wig or false beard which might fall off. Oh, he's shrewd, all right, shrewd and far seeing; but like all of his brand, he makes the little slips that are his undoing."

"Uh-huh, with *El Halcón* on his trail," the sheriff agreed dryly. "He would have made a nice haul tonight if it wasn't for you."

"And I think," Slade said, "that if he had been successful, we would have seen the last of 'Juan Covelo' and Gus Hansen hereabouts. He would have very likely finished off his three companions and pulled out, loaded. I figure he'll do it if he can manage to make one more good haul. Well, we'll see."

The makeshift train with its puffing yard engine reached El Paso. The horses were unloaded and stabled. Slade and the sheriff paused at the latter's office.

"I told Bob to have those two carcasses brought here," Hart said. "We'll lay 'em out for inspection, and of course there'll be an inquest. Tomorrow afternoon, the chances are. Now what?"

"Wait until the bodies arrive so we can give them a once-over," Slade said. "Chances are it'll be just a waste of time, but we mustn't miss any bets."

"Right," said the sheriff. "I think I hear him coming with 'em now."

As Slade expected, the bodies revealed nothing he considered of significance, save a rather large sum of money for such specimens to be carrying.

"An outlaw leader must keep his men supplied with ready cash if he hopes to hold them," Slade observed.

"More for the county treasury," the sheriff said cheerfully as he dropped the *dinero* in a drawer. "Next?"

"Next I'm going to amble down to Pablo's place; he'll still be open."

"A good notion," agreed Hart, "But be careful; I think you've had enough excitement for one night."

"I think so, too," the Ranger agreed and took his departure.

Pablo's *cantina* was open, and Carmen was awaiting him.

"At least you got back before daylight," she said. "We heard about the wreck, and I know very well you were mixed up in it somehow. Tell me what happened."

Slade proceeded to do so. She sighed, and shook her curly head.

"Keeping company with you is like riding a Gulf hurricane," she declared. "But," she flashed him a smile, "I always rather liked hurricanes. I'm going to the kitchen and have something to eat prepared for you; you must be starved."

"I could stand a bite about now," he admitted. "Nice of you to look after me like you do."

"You don't deserve it, but I can't help myself," she retorted and bounced off to the kitchen.

Pablo and Gordo Allende joined Slade and he repeated the story for their edification.

"And a lot of the credit for frustrating the attempt goes to Gordo," he concluded.

"It is the pleasure to serve *El Halcón*," Gordo instantly replied. "Here comes Carmen with the something special for you. I hope she doesn't fall down with it."

Slade ate his much belated dinner with relish. The east was flushing with dawn and Pablo was putting up the shutters when he and Carmen left the *cantina* together.

19 . . .

The inquest the following afternoon yielded no results. Nobody admitted knowing the dead outlaws who, said the verdict, got just what was coming to them. Slade was commended for doing a first class chore, the sheriff advised to run down the other two hellions without delay. Which caused that peace officer to swear under his mustache.

"I've a notion to throw Hansen into the calaboose on general principles," he growled to Slade.

"Would be just a waste of time," the Ranger replied. "'I still have no case that would stand up in court; all just conjecture. I believe my deductions are sound, but I can't prove them. We'll just have to wait till he makes another move and hope we'll get the goods on him. Now it's up to him to play. I'm confident he will, all right, and before long. I imagine he is getting a bit frantic, which may cloud his judgment and cause him to do something foolish, although he certainly has not so far."

The sheriff got busy on some paper work. Slade strolled about the town, wracking his brains for some clue as to what would be Hansen's next move. He believed this depended on how perturbed the saloonkeeper was and how many followers he still had or would be able to enlist. The man who looked like a seaman might be the only one of the bunch left, but of that Slade was not sure. The shrewd outlaw leader might have decided that four men were sufficient for the chore of wrecking and robbing the Limited and, if he had really made up his mind to pull out, might have reasoned that three would be easier to dispose of than a larger number. For Slade was firmly convinced that Hansen had had no intention of sharing his big haul with his followers. The callous devil had not the slightest regard for human life and the extinction of the three would not have bothered him in the least. And Slade believed he would have been able to accomplish it. Well, all he could do at the moment was wait for Hansen to make a move.

Finally he turned into Texas Street and walked slowly to

the edge of town. For some time he stood gazing in a north-easterly direction toward the Hueco Mountains glowing in the red rays of the setting sun. In the lurid light beating upon them, their stony crests seemed to drip blood. The blood of the many who had died violently in the shadow of their crags. There the dawn men had held high revel under the orbed moon. There the screaming victim stretched on the stone of sacrifice had shrunk from the flash of the descending knife. There the Apache had stalked his quarry, arrow on the string. There the outlaw hid, the smuggler handed over his wares to the ready buyer. The home of dark deeds and ruthless cruelty. Even now as in the days of savage men and savage beasts. The Huecos were ageless, their canyons and gorges still sheltering evil.

And Slade was convinced that somewhere amid that desolation Gus Hansen had a secret hide-out where he would feel safe from pursuit and might well bide his time, should that become necessary, until he was ready to pull out of the section.

Till the shadows crept up the slopes and the mountain crests dulled to somber gray *El Halcón* stood and gazed, making his plans that might well end in a rendezvous with death.

With the darkness closing about him like the folds of a shroud, he turned and walked back to the lights and the bustle, the voices and the laughter of El Paso.

Gradually his somber mood lifted and he was humming a gay tune under his breath when he turned south toward the river and Pablo's *cantina*, where bright eyes and smiling lips awaited.

"So you didn't go gallivanting off somewhere and are really here!" Carmen greeted him.

"I am," he replied. "And I'm hungry, and I want to dance with you."

"First you eat," she said. "A hungry man is not good company, on a dance-floor or—elsewhere."

"Hmmm!" he commented. She blushed, made a face at him and hurried to the kitchen.

Pablo came over and occupied the vacant chair. "Gordo and I examined those *ladrones* with care, as we promised to do," he announced. "We knew them not."

"Thanks just the same," Slade replied. "Had you recognized them it might have helped!"

Privately he felt that at the moment it did not matter with whom the dead outlaws might have associated. He knew his man. Now his only problem was to drop a loop on him.

How? He had only a vague notion that was utterly dependent on developments.

Developments of a surprising nature were soon to come.

Slade enjoyed a leisurely dinner, with Carmen for company. Then they had several dances together before the girl retired to the back room to finish some work. Slade remained at the table, smoking and sipping coffee.

He was comfortable and relaxed. There was nothing he could do at present and he decided to take it easy and enjoy himself.

"I feel like just doing nothing," he told Carmen when she returned. She shot him a glance through her lashes.

"Nothing?"

"Well, almost nothing," he qualified. Carmen smiled and dimpled.

The following afternoon, Slade strolled down Santa Fe Street, eventually entering The Tank. Joe Brian, grinning, hurried to greet him.

"Shake hands with an up-and-coming businessman," he chuckled. "That is if I haven't spread myself too thin."

"Now what do you mean by that?" Slade asked.

"I'm expanding," Brian explained. "Yesterday I bought another place."

"The dickens you did!" Slade exclaimed. "What place?"

"The Lemming Inn."

"The Lemming Inn!" Slade repeated, staring at the saloonkeeper.

"That's right," said Brian. "Gus Hansen came in and said he aimed to sell and go back to California where he had friends and relations. Made me what I considered a good proposition. I've been doing very well since I opened up here, and after paying Richard Gird what I owed him, I had some money left. So I went to the bank, put my cards on the table and borrowed what I needed to close the deal. Hansen seemed anxious to sell in a hurry. Said he'd very likely take the night train west. Reckon he did. Haven't seen him around today. Sit down, we're going to celebrate. Waiter! Bring champagne."

As they sipped the wine, Brian asked, "What do you think?"

"I think you made a good buy," Slade replied. "The Lemming Inn is a good holding, and this town is growing fast."

"Glad you think so," said Brian. "I value your opinion. Fill 'em up again!"

He chattered on about his enterprise, but Slade was silent, digesting the unexpected information, thinking hard. He did not believe that Hansen took the night train to California, although perhaps he would eventually return there, if he was not stopped. He wondered what the shrewd devil was planning. Well, he'd very likely learn soon, and doubtless it would be something unpleasant.

"My head bartender will run this place," said Brian. "He's a good man, and he wants to buy a piece of it. Expect I'll let him have it."

"A good idea," Slade said. "Then he'll take a more active interest in the business."

"So I figure," nodded Brian. He poured a final glass of champagne. "I don't care much for this bubble water," he confessed, "but I figured it the proper drink for a celebration."

"Very fitting," Slade agreed. "Here's to success in your venture, and I'm confident you'll achieve it."

"Thanks," answered Brian. "I'm glad to hear you say it, for as I said before, like it seems everybody else does, I put great faith in your judgment."

They drank the toast, shook hands again and parted.

Without delay, Slade headed for the sheriff's office, where he acquainted Hart with the unexpected development.

"So the hellion really is pulling out," the sheriff snorted. "Blast him, anyhow! Is he going to slide out of the loop?"

"He is, unless I can do something to prevent him, and in a hurry," Slade replied grimly. "I'm of the opinion that he is very likely to pull something before he trails his twine, and I haven't the slightest notion what. I'm going to wait one more day, gambling that I'm right in my surmise, then I'm going to play a hunch, a real long shot that could pay off big."

"But watch your step," Hart cautioned. "Would be just like him to make a try at doing you in before he leaves. I've a notion he isn't feeling very kindly toward you about now."

"He's tried it a few times, without any luck, so I guess I can take a chance," Slade returned cheerfully. The sheriff growled.

"Yes, I guess you can," he said. "I've a feeling some particular devil goes along with you who takes care of his own."

"Not a bad sort of devil to have around," Slade countered. "How about some coffee?"

"I got a pot on the stove in the back office," Hart replied. "I'll rustle a couple of cups."

Slade did not take the sheriff's warning as lightly as he pretended to, for he did not underestimate Gus Hansen, alias Juan Covelo. Too often he had demonstrated his streak of vindictive cruelty. If the man who called himself Covelo could possibly manage it, he, Slade, would not die a swift and merciful death, but a lingering agony with the mocking *Buenas noches, Señor!* the last words to reach his ears.

The coffee was quickly forthcoming and both partook of it in silence, each busy with his own thoughts, the subject of which was the same—what the devil would be Hansen's next move.

They would soon find out.

It was the sheriff who had the news to impart the following morning when Slade visited him.

"He did it," he said. "Oh, it was him, all right. The Welston Mining Company's office safe busted open and cleaned of better than thirty thousand dollars. Combination drilled out slick as a whistle. They found the night watchman with his head split open. Guess he was lucky not to get a knife in his back."

"Badly hurt?" Slade asked with concern. Hart shook his head.

"Not too bad, I guess. Skull fracture, but Doc McChesney says he'll pull him through, and you can depend on old Doc. Now I reckon the hellion will really trail his twine."

"Yes, but not right away, I believe," Slade replied. "I've a notion he'll lay low for a few days, until things cool down. At least that's what I'm banking on."

"And you figure you know where to find him?"

"Sort of, like knowing where to find a certain tick on a sheep's back," Slade answered. "Not easy, but if you keep on going over the sheep's back you'll eventually find the tick. In other words, I think I know the general locality where he can be found."

"The Hueco Mountains?"

"That's right, somewhere in the Huecos."

"That's a lot of territory to comb," grunted Hart.

"Yes, but I have something to go on," Slade said. "I am of the opinion that they were heading Heth Jackson's wide-looped cows to the hide-out. Perhaps I can pick up the trail. Anyhow, I'm going to try."

"You should let me go with you," Hart suggested. Slade shook his head.

"I feel I can handle this chore better by myself," he said. "Everything depends on getting the jump on the hellions and I think I'll have a greater chance to do that alone. In my opinion that former seaman is all that's left of the bunch, so I'll only have two to deal with. Perhaps only one, if Hansen manages to do him in quickly, which I'm sure he will sooner or later."

"Maybe you're right," sighed the sheriff. "You always seem to know what you're about, but I'm scairt you're taking one helluva chance."

"All in the day's work," Slade returned lightly.

"Going to start right away?" Hart asked. Slade again shook his head.

"I think I'd better wait until late afternoon," he decided. "It will be dark or close to it when I reach that canyon through which they drove the rustled cows. I'll make camp there for the night and get an early start in the morning."

"Figure there's any chance somebody here in town might be keeping tabs on you?"

"Highly unlikely, I'd say," Slade replied. "As I said, I think there's only one of the bunch left. But if there is somebody, I anticipate no difficulty in throwing him off the trail. In fact, I'd rather welcome such a contingency, for the fellow might lead me to the hide-out. Little chance of it, however."

The sun was well down the western slant of the sky when Slade got the rig on Shadow. After making sure that his saddle pouches held ample provisions for a night out, plus a surrounding of oats for his mount, he rode out of town. He did not turn east, but west, constantly glancing over his shoulder. Shadow ambled along at a fair pace.

He drew rein when he reached a rise and studied the back track. Confident he was not wearing a tail, he made a wide detour and regained the trail some miles east of El Paso.

Sunset crimsoned the western sky, the dusk descended. Slade rode on steadily. Soon there was only the wan glow of the stars to light the way, but with the plainsman's unerring instinct for distance and direction, he turned north at the right point and ultimately reached the narrow canyon where he camped the night of the widelooping of Heth Jackson's cattle.

Tonight the weather was fine; an overhang provided all the shelter required. After making Shadow comfortable, he rolled up in his blanket with his saddle for a pillow and soon was fast asleep.

20 . . .

The first flush of dawn found Slade preparing breakfast for himself and the horse. After eating and cleaning up, he mounted and set out on his hazardous quest, following the route taken by the purloined cows, which proved to be an old Indian track. It was very faint, at times obliterated altogether, but curved steadily into the foothills of the Huecos.

He rode slowly, scanning the ground, watching for broken twigs or dislodged stones, convinced that horses and cattle had passed this way not too long ago. He constantly studied the sky for that betrayer of the hunted, smoke.

Mile after mile he rode, following the track into a narrow gorge where the marks left by cattle and horses were quite plain.

"This is beginning to look too darn easy," he told Shadow. "The hellions didn't appear to take any thought that they might be tracked. Right now a child could follow the trail; but I've got a prime notion this won't last."

It didn't. Before long the gorge opened into a space of level ground flanked on either side by tall hills. This continued for half a mile or so. Then abruptly the trail of horses and cattle swerved to enter an even narrower canyon with a rocky floor; here the passing stock left no sign. Other canyons opened into the one he had just entered, running this way and that, and all with the adamantine flooring which displayed no scar of hoof or horse's iron. Not even the eyes of *El Halcón* could detect a trace of passage that would tell him he was on the right track.

Nevertheless, he persisted doggedly as the hours wore on, exploring gorge after gorge, with no results. The sun crossed the zenith, started down the long slant of the western sky. Thoroughly disgusted by this lack of luck, Slade pulled to a halt, rolled and lighted a cigarette and considered the situation. Soon it would be dark and what already seemed to be a senseless quest would undoubtedly be altogether so.

119

Shadow snorted derisively. His rider tried to look grand and confident but felt that the attitude did not impress. Then he stared about as if taking counsel with the heavens, devoutly hoping that the heavens, or something, would respond to his mute appeal. As a matter of fact, they obligingly did.

Rising through the crystal air, topping the stony crags and merging with the deeper blue of the sky was a thin blue line, barely visible but continuing steadily. He estimated its source as about a mile ahead and slightly to the left; and the rock walled canyon curved gradually to the left.

"See?" he exclaimed exultantly to the horse. "Told you I knew what I was about."

"Just pure luck," the answering snort scoffed. "If you'd kept going another hundred feet without giving me a chance to catch my breath, you wouldn't have been able to see it."

Which was so; the configuration of the cliffs was such that a little farther on the pale streamer would have been invisible, and Slade had just about decided to turn back and explore some other gorge that might look more promising.

"Okay, you win," he surrendered. "'But just the same we're on the right track. Now we'll amble along and see what we can find. I'm willing to bet a hatful of pesos that smoke comes from the chimney of some old prospector or hunter's cabin, and that the cabin is the hole-up we've been hunting all day. Let's go!"

He sent the horse forward, slowly, every sense at hair-trigger alert. If the smoke really did mark Covelo's secret hang-out a slip on his part would be fatal; if the outlaws heard him coming they'd be ready for him with the advantage all on their side.

The canyon continued, walled by tall cliffs, still curving slightly. Abruptly it straightened out, directly in line with the faint trickle of smoke.

Ahead, clumps of thicket were in evidence, for the rock floor was replaced by earth. Slade's pulses quickened as again he noted the indubitable evidence of the recent passage of cattle and horses.

"We're on the right track!" he exulted. "Looks like the showdown."

He slowed Shadow's gait still more, peering and listening. No sound broke the afternoon hush. There was no sign of movement. He reasoned that the outlaws had very likely been sleeping and had awakened to prepare a meal.

A little farther and he pulled to a halt at the edge of a thicket somewhat broader and denser than any that had gone before. He dared not ride farther, for the click of Shadow's hoofs sounded loud in the great stillness.

"Here's where you take it easy for a while," he told his mount. "I'll be with you soon, I hope."

Dismounting, he led the horse into the clump of brush. Scanty grass grew between the trunks, so he flipped the bit out to enable the animal to graze.

"And no singing songs or straying into the open," he warned, dropping the split reins to the ground as a hint not to do any ambling.

He wasn't much worried on either score, however; Shadow was a very silent horse and he knew when he was meant to stay put.

Very slowly, Slade eased ahead on foot, hugging the shadow of the cliffs, flitting from brush clump to brush clump, pausing often to peer and listen.

Still no sound broke the silence, and his watchful eyes could detect no movement. He realized he couldn't go much farther, for the canyon proved to be a box. Finally he paused in the fringe of a final bristle of thicket and peered through the leaves and twigs.

Directly ahead was the end wall of the box, less than two score yards distant. Between where he stood and the end wall was an open space that showed many signs of cattle that had been held in close herd. But nowhere was there a cabin, a shack, or even a lean-to. And the faint spiral of smoke appeared to rise from the crest of the end wall, which was much shorter than the side cliffs.

"What in blazes!" he exclaimed under his breath. "Where the devil are they?"

His gaze roved back and forth across the sheer wall of rock which was now shadowy since the sun had sunk behind the side cliffs to the west.

Abruptly his gaze centered, centered on a dark opening at the base of the end cliff. Undoubtedly it was the mouth of one of the caves which honeycombed the region.

Now what to do? A cave was the hang-out and the devils were holed up in there; and had a fire going, the smoke escaping by way of a fissure in the cave roof.

Easing back into the growth a little deeper against the chance of watching eyes, he considered the situation, which was dubious, to put it mildly. To reach the cave mouth he would be forced to traverse an open space. Even hugging the cliff wall would be frightfully hazardous. Should anyone come to the mouth of the cave he would assuredly be spotted, with the spotter in the semi-gloom and himself in the light; a settin' quail. Long and earnestly, he debated the problem which confronted him, concluding that his only chance was to get into the cave unobserved and shoot it out with the hellions.

A large order, everything taken into account, but so far as he could see, the only solution. That or wait till night, under cover of which the pair might well escape him. He'd have to take a long chance hoping luck would be with him.

One angle of the situation appeared to be in his favor. The fact that the outlaws had a fire going appeared to indicate that they were preparing a meal and their attention would be occupied by the chore. Also, the cave seemed fairly deep. Otherwise he would see the glow of the fire, even had it already burned down to a bed of coals suitable for cooking. And no sound reached his keen ears, another indication that the opening in the cliff was not shallow.

For another moment he hesitated, as one is apt to do before taking an irrevocable step. Oh, the devil! He had a chore to do. So get busy and do it. He drew a deep breath, slid from his place of concealment and glided along the base of the cliff, straining ears and eyes for sound or movement.

Nothing happened. He reached the end wall with a feeling of great relief. Now the odds wouldn't be so much against him. Listening and peering, he eased along the wall until he was within a couple of feet of the cave mouth. Again he hesitated. Now he felt sure he could hear, very faintly, a murmur of voices, then a tinny rattle as if a plate or a cup was struck against the rock. They were in there, all right, and it looked like he was right in surmising that they were busy preparing a meal.

Slade experienced a surge of renewed confidence. Looked like he might well catch the devils settin'. Hands to his gun butts, he edged around to the opening and slipped into the cave, and halted.

Now he could see that about thirty feet farther on, the cave curved rather sharply, and at the curve was a glow of light; and the murmur of voices had abruptly loudened. Yes, the devils were in there, and apparently busy and showing no signs of alarm.

Step by cautious step he eased ahead, reached the apex of the turn. The light had strengthened and the movements of the men about the fire were plainly apparent. One more stride and he was around the bend and in Juan Covelo's secret hide-out.

Beyond the curve the cave widened somewhat, and the space had been fitted up very comfortably. There were bunks built against the wall, a rude stone fireplace in which the fire glowed, two bracket lamps pegged to the wall, several home-made chairs and a homemade table. On shelves was a store of staple provisions. The furnishings looked very old and doubtless had been thrown together by a former inhabitant of the cave years before. Beyond, the tunnel again narrowed and stretched into darkness.

Bending over the fire, manipulating cooking utensils, were two men. The hair of one glinted golden in the light of the lamps.

Slade opened his lips to speak, and at that instant a horse, unseen in the gloom of the continuing tunnel, gave a loud and frightened snort.

Instantly the two outlaws surged erect and whirled toward the mouth of the cave with startled exclamations. Slade's voice rang out, "Elevate! You're covered! In the name of the State of Texas—"

With a yell of rage, Gus Hansen went for his gun; his companion, lurching forward, also grabbed for his iron.

Slade drew and shot, left and right, aiming at Hanson. But even as he pulled the trigger, the other man leaped forward again and landed squarely in front of the outlaw leader. He gave a strangled cry as the Ranger's slugs hammered his body. Hansen's gun blazed and the bullet fanned Slade's face as he slewed sideways. A second shot ripped through the sleeve of his shirt, graining the flesh of his arm, nearly knocking him off balance with the shock. Hansen's companion crumpled up like a sack of old clothes, but slowly enough to give Hansen opportunity. He whirled, darted into the gloom of the tunnel and vanished from sight.

Slade bounded forward, leaped over the still twitching body of the dying outlaw, rushed in pursuit, and slammed into a horse invisible in the darkness of the tunnel. He caromed off the frightened animal, staggered, reeled and took a glorious header, hitting the rock floor with a force that knocked all the breath from his lungs and for a moment paralyzed his limbs.

Gasping an oath, he floundered, rolled over, scrambled erect. Ahead, fading in the distance, he could just hear the click of Hansen's boots on the floor of the cave. His strength surging back, he raced after the fleeing outlaw chief. The

click of heels grew a little louder; evidently he was slowly
closing the distance. He did not risk a shot, for the flash of
the gun would reveal his own position. The infernal hole
couldn't go on forever and eventually Hansen must come to
a halt; then they'd shoot it out.

21 . . .

Slade's heart was pounding, his breath was labored, his legs were beginning to tremble a little. He estimated he had covered fully a quarter of a mile at top speed with the floor of the cave steadily rising to form a gentle slope up which he toiled. And Hansen appeared to be holding his own.

Abruptly the blackness ahead grayed. The tunnel curved a little. Another instant and his eyes were dazzled by a beam of light that poured through an opening in the west wall of the cave. He saw Hansen flash through the beam of light and again vanish from his sight. Instinctively he slowed his pace a little. The opening in the cave wall must lead to the outside; perhaps Hansen was there waiting for him. He slowed a little more, reached the fissure which he saw opened onto a narrow ledge; Hansen was not visible.

Anxious to get it over with one way or another, Slade darted through the opening, guns ready for action, and rocked back on his heels.

The ledge clung to the side of the cliff, rising steeply. And nearly two hundred yards ahead, he saw Hansen. His heart leaped as he raced in pursuit, for he saw something else. Only a few yards in front of the outlaw leader the ledge ended, its edge standing out clear against the sky. Hansen would have to turn and shoot it out.

"Showdown!" Slade exulted.

It wasn't. Hansen turned his head. Back to the straining Ranger drifted a mocking, *"Buenas noches, Señor!"*

Slade swore unbelievingly as the outlaw leaped into space and for the third time vanished from sight.

Once more Slade slowed his pace. Looked like Hansen had decided to commit suicide; but perhaps not. Maybe he was crouched on a shelf or bench a few feet below, waiting for *El Halcón* to poke his head over the edge. Oh, the devil with him! He increased his stride and a moment later reached the edge to pause, staring.

Some fifty feet below the sheer drop from the ledge was a stream that gushed from under the cliff wall, to all appearances a deep stream. About two hundred yards farther on it abruptly changed direction to disappear between stands of growth. And at the beginning of the turn the sunlight, reflected downward from a passing cloud, gleamed on something golden—Gus Hansen's hair!

And even as Slade glared in baffled fury, the white blur of the swimming outlaw's face turned toward him. A derisive hand was waved and for the fourth and last time, Hansen vanished from his sight.

For a moment, so great was his wrath, he was tempted to plunge in and swim in pursuit. But common sense told him it would be the act of a stark staring lunatic, just a gory way to commit suicide. Hansen could leave the stream beyond the bend, wherever he saw fit, and the advantage would be utterly on his side. No, he might as well admit it, he had been neatly outwitted.

Juan Covelo was unfinished business!

Thoroughly disgusted, he made his way back down the ledge and through the cave to the hang-out, where the body of the slain outlaw lay. A glance told him the fellow was the man of seafaring appearance, the last of Covelo's bunch.

Dragging the body to one side, he secured a bracket lamp and took a look at the horse he stumbled over. With a companion it was tethered to a peg driven in the cave wall. There were feed boxes also pegged to the rock and both animals, recovered from their fright, were contentedly munching oats, a sack of which stood nearby. So he retrieved Shadow and treated him to a feeding.

On the fire, which had burned down to a few coals, was a skillet of bacon and eggs, not too badly scorched, and a pot of steaming coffee. There were loaves of bread on a shelf. Breaking out one, he proceeded to enjoy a hearty meal. After eating he smoked a cigarette and then took stock of his surroundings.

Near the fireplace were a couple of plumped-out saddle pouches. They proved to be crammed with money, evidently the loot from the Welston Mining Company's office safe. He did not take the trouble to count it.

The dead owlhoot's pockets divulged several packets of big bills. Doubtless Covelo had carried a like amount in his clothes. So he was well heeled and could purchase a horse and rig, if he didn't take one from some lone rider, after a little genteel murder, and make good his get-away. Yes, Co-velo was unfinished business.

Oh, well! There'd come another time. He'd bob up some-place. And the day wasn't a total loss. The last of the bunch done for and most of the stolen money recovered. Might as well take a philosophical view of the business. He built up the fire, stretched out on one of the bunks and went to sleep.

Dawn found him up and preparing some breakfast. Then he roped the dead man to one of the horses and, leading the animals, set out on the long ride to El Paso, arriving there just before sunset.

After depositing the body in the sheriff's office and caring for the horses, he regaled Hart with an account of his ad-ventures and misadventures.

"The hellion either always got the breaks or made them, mostly made them," he concluded. "I was outsmarted, and that's all there is to it."

"Uh-huh, and Veck Sosna got the breaks, for a while, but ended getting his comeuppance," said the sheriff. "You did everything a man could do, so don't go blaming yourself. Covelo will get his, sooner or later, no doubt in my mind as to that."

"Here's hoping," Slade replied cheerfully."But he'll take some catching; he's a shrewd article if there ever was one, and with a hair-trigger brain that instantly takes advantage of opportunity. Just as he did when his companion took the slugs I intended for him. The fellow reeling and staggering in front of him before he fell gave Hansen the split second of opportunity he needed, and he took advantage of it, diving into that crack instead of shooting it out with me. Familiar with the lay of the land, he knew exactly where he was going and knew that if he could make the crest of that ledge ahead of me, he'd give me the slip. Which is just what he did.

"Yes, shrewd and farseeing. He carefully built up the Juan Covelo myth and had everybody looking for a swarthy, swag-gering half Indian with a taste for the bizarre and wanton cruelty. I'm of the opinion that his cruelty, such as pegging a man over an ant hill, was not cruelty in the accepted sense of the word, but part of the cold, carefully thought out build up of the character, Juan Covelo. Hansen himself being the very antithesis, in appearance and action, of the supposed-to-be Covelo. Yes, he'll show up somewhere else—his sort never quits—but, in my opinion, as something totally different from what he appeared to be in this section.

"He probably did," Slade agreed. "Well, be seeing you. I'm dropping in at Pablo's *cantina* later."

"A good notion," said Hart. "How's the iittle gal?"

"She's okay," Slade replied. "Pretty as ever."

Sheriff Hart chuckled as he watched the Ranger's tall form pass through the door.

"Got a notion he'll be huntin' for excuses to visit El Paso," he observed to his pipe. "Well, he could do worse."